Tales from a Florida Fish Camp

and Other Tidbits of Swamp Rat Philosophy

Jack Montrose

Pineapple Press
Sarasota, Florida

Dedicated to no one in particular and to all the old swamp rats in general, with gratitude to the innocent public.

Inquiries should be addressed to:

Pineapple Press, Inc.
P.O. Box 3889
Sarasota, Florida 34230
www.pineapplepress.com

Library of Congress Cataloging-in-Publication Data

Montrose, Jack.
Tales from a Florida fish camp / Jack Montrose.
p. cm.
ISBN 1-56164-276-2 (pbk. : alk. paper)
1. Fishing—Florida—Saint Johns River—Anecdotes. 2. Fishing lodges—Florida—Saint Johns River—Anecdotes. I. Title.
SH483 .M66 2003
799.1'1'097591—dc21

2002014305

First Edition
10 9 8 7 6 5 4 3 2 1

Design by Shé Sicks
Printed in the United States of America

Contents

Foreword

"Someone should write a book!" That statement is made pretty much every time a group of us old river rats get together and rehash fish camp happenings. We are in total agreement that someone should write a book but time kept passing by and the book never appeared. We also thought there was a void in the recent history of life and happenings on the St. Johns River. This is a serious oversight that should be corrected.

Now, I most certainly am not a writer. Where I went to school you graduated after completing twelve years of schooling, or upon reaching the age of thirty-six, whichever came first. Be that as it may, since it is now evident that no one else is going to take the initiative, here I go with *Tales from a Florida Fish Camp.*

I have been a fish camp regular since 1965, and over that relatively brief period of time have observed enough uncommon events to fill volumes. Of course, many occurrences are not printable and others would be denied by all involved, but we can put up with that. I simply can't tell you about the man and his wife having a private demolition derby in the parking lot, him with his airboat and her with a pickup truck. Unfortunately I must also omit the episode about the casket (you wouldn't believe it anyway). No matter, even with all the exclusions there is still enough material for many books.

Tales from a Florida Fish Camp is written for the sole purpose of documenting and preserving some of the events that have occurred in the area we like to consider our part of the St. Johns River. In reality, these stories do not come from one fish camp but from four. I'm sorry to say that only two of these remain in operation. Admittedly, to most folks the demise of a fish camp is of absolutely no significance, but to others, like us old regulars, it is nothing less than the loss of a historic, irreplaceable shrine—only the more reason to record adventures and misadventures that will never happen again.

Most of the described episodes date back several years. Perhaps I am getting old and grouchy, but modern happenings do not seem to contain the totally innocent humor that once prevailed. For that matter, I am often bewildered by modern-day thinking. We always cleaned our fish on the edge of the lake where the inedible residue was chucked in the water—total recycling if you will. Humans ate the fillets, and fish, turtles, and gators ate the rest. Nothing was wasted. As a word of warning, this is no longer allowed. A person can be charged with littering and feeding alligators, both rather serious crimes with hefty fines. Apparently fish-cleaning residue is now destined for the already-overloaded landfill.

Last names are not normally used in these short stories. If you know the people being discussed, the last name is not needed, and if you didn't know them, their last name is of no significance anyway. Besides, this may allow a culprit to deny involvement and shift the blame to some innocent individual with the same first name.

Fish Camps

W*ITHOUT DIGGING BACK TOO FAR INTO HISTORY,* let's take a look at the various St. Johns River fish camps located near Melbourne during the mid-1960s. Earlier, the same basic fish camps had existed, but most had operated under different names. Sweetwater Camp has retained its name, but who remembers the St. Johns River Fishing Camp or Lake Washington Sporting Camp? Uncle Bill's Fishing Camp more or less lost its identity as a camp and simply became Uncle Bill's.

In the '60s there were four fish camps. Each had its own following of fishermen, airboaters, and other folks who, though they didn't participate much in fishing or boating, still showed up regularly and were considered part of the group. All were basically good people with more interest in nature and the outdoors than what could be found in meeting places and watering holes uptown. Some may find it interesting that I-95 had been completed, the population of Melbourne was 40,234, the population of Palm Bay was 6,927, and Melbourne International Airport was called J. F. Kennedy Memorial Airport.

Lake Washington Resort was the most extensive of the camps, with several cabins, a store that also served as a beer bar, a launch ramp, more than forty covered boat stalls, and what was called the "cook shack." Maybe the term "resort" was a bit misleading; there were numerous phone calls inquiring about tennis, golf, horseback riding, and other silly non–fish camp facilities.

Often the scene of huge crowds for fundraising benefits, the camp was originally operated by Cotton and Mary Leaf. Later,

Jane Leaf and Lois Callahan were the proprietors, eventually selling the camp to Jack Harnish. Harnish owned the camp for a period of years before selling it to the county in 1990. Lake Washington Marina, originally owned and operated by the Lombards, passed through various hands and was renamed a few times before its demise.

Sweetwater, at one time called Lake Hellen Blazes Camp, was operated by Vic Woodling then later owned and operated by Kim Hanna and his family. Though not an overly active place, Sweetwater still serves as a fish camp and home base for a number of boaters.

Camp Holly, during the period when most of these events occurred, was owned and operated by Henry and Ruby Hollingsworth. Henry once mentioned that when he bought the camp from a Mr. Wall, the entire stock consisted of one soft drink and two boxes of fishing worms. Obviously, the camp at that time was no beehive of activity. Later, the camp was owned by John and Lynne Cataldo, then by Bob Mitchell. Camp Holly, currently owned and operated by Darold and Pat Hite, still serves as a fish camp with boats, bait, and tackle but is most noted for airboat rides.

That area of the St. Johns River shown on the map on page 97, Lake Winder to Lake Hellen Blazes, was generally considered home territory to local fishermen and boaters. As the crow flies, the distance from the southern end of Hellen Blazes to the northern end of Lake Winder is about twenty miles. However, since we've never found an airboat or kicker boat that could fly like a crow, the actual distance is considerably more, maybe twenty-seven miles.

There were thousands of acres of marsh available to airboaters during periods of reasonable water levels in this area. Fishing was so outstanding there was little reason for fishermen to venture far from a fish camp. A beautiful, wild, natural area teeming with all native forms of wildlife and fish, the area was thoroughly enjoyed and appreciated by the relatively few number of individuals who, at the time, took a genuine interest in its welfare.

Camps and Shacks

CAMPS AND SHACKS WERE NOT NUMEROUS and certainly did not feature all the conveniences of modern-day living. Four walls, a floor, and a roof were enough to start with, then human nature normally took over to make many improvements. Remote hard-to-reach locations were preferred, lending an air of mystery. Indeed, many fish camp regulars might often hear the names Sugar Shack and Gator Den without ever seeing the camps or knowing their locations.

Building a camp was not easy since everything had to be transported by boat and the construction done with hand tools. Since old river rats were seldom blessed with a surplus of money, most building materials were scrounged—obtained in any manner besides paying for them. This process in itself was often quite interesting, but we'd best not identify individuals or circumstances. ("Why are all these full sheets of plywood in the scrap heap?" "Who cares? Just load them on the truck. We can use them at the camp.")

Originally, camps were never locked and canned foods were left in the event someone might need to take refuge. Many of us have ducked into a camp to sit out a storm; others with boat trouble sometimes were forced to stay the night. It was common practice to replace any food you used doubly the next time you were in the vicinity.

Yes, that's the way it was, but then things changed. Vandalism became prevalent, and ranchers definitely disliked the fact that camps were located close to their land.

Bob Fortenberry's camp saw considerable activity and good times galore. Now, if my memory serves me correctly, Bob (sometimes called R.O. or Pop) had a well, sometimes planted a small garden, and kept the grass mowed. Senseless vandalism was the downfall of Bob's camp. He might arrive at the camp after a few days' absence to find his supplies not used but simply destroyed. Furnishings were also destroyed, and there was often a big mess to clean up. Then some idiot, unable to find a better target, simply riddled the lawn mower with a high-powered rifle. Right or wrong, incidents of this nature were usually attributed to unsupervised youngsters. We'll never know for certain who they were, but obviously they were the type of people who would rather destroy than enjoy.

Jeff and I built a small shack deep in the trees on Little Sawgrass Lake. It had only the basics, with one large, hinged window, and was made entirely from scrap material with the exception of a roll of roofing. The location was so enjoyable, however, we later added a large porch for invited visitors. We searched for several days to find the perfect site, a place along a brush-covered trail where the shack could not be seen from the water. Built during the winter, when there were few people out, I would stop hammering when even a distant motor was heard. The secret hideaway was a total success. Some people had seen us hauling materials and knew we had a camp, but try as they might they couldn't find it.

The camp was weatherproof but, sorry to say, definitely not mosquito-proof. Not long after we finished construction, we tried sleeping there and found it impossible. It was OK in the daytime, but at sunset the mosquitoes took over. We eventually gave up, moved our boat to the center of Lake Sawgrass, where there was a slight breeze, chucked the anchor overboard, and had a reasonable night's sleep.

With early summer we received an unexpected and pleasant surprise. Hundreds, perhaps thousands, of birds established a rookery overhead. Now, in addition to the other critters we had enjoyed watching in their undisturbed habitat, there was a multitude of ibises, herons, egrets, and others building nests and raising young. Can anyone describe the sounds of a large bird rookery? The best I can do is to say there were constant squabbles, each and every bird defending its small domain and fussing at neighbors because of intrusions or near intrusions. It is interesting that these species of birds, other than at nesting time, are mostly silent.

A rookery does not quiet down with nightfall. The birds are packed in so closely that any movement on the part of one disturbs those nearby and the squabble continues. The mosquito problem partially solved with sprays and repellents, we again stayed overnight. Sleeping in a bird rookery is something few people have experienced. The unusual noises might keep you awake for awhile but then will lull you to sleep. Noises of nature are that way, quite unlike a neighbor's loud boom box or roaring automobiles.

It seems every rookery has a gator cruising in the water below. We saw several small gators, but soon a large, boss gator, maybe ten feet long, took over. Nowhere to be seen when we quietly slipped in and tied up the boat, he would soon appear. Resenting our intrusion, the gator would glide around, looking everything over at close range. Then, apparently satisfied, he would resume his patrol under the many trees. Only under such conditions can a person appreciate how a gator, even a large one, can move through the water without creating even a ripple. In my opinion, a gator in his element is the most stealthy creature on earth.

A momma otter raised five little ones nearby, and, though they couldn't actually be considered pets, they certainly became very friendly. When we first saw them, the youngsters were perhaps half as large as the mother and extremely skittish. This changed as time passed. Whenever I spotted the family, I would stop fishing and watch the playful creatures. Probably as curious about me as I was about them, after a while they became accustomed to my boat and so trusting they would come when I whistled. This became almost a daily ritual—the little ones swimming around the boat while momma stayed off a ways, fussing at their carelessness. Other boaters thought they had to chase the critters for a close-up look, and, when this happened, the entire family simply went into hiding. There was no doubt they recognized my boat and my whistle. Much more observant than you would expect, they would not hesitate to come to my boat when I was alone but were reluctant if I had someone with me.

Momma eventually decided the porch at the shack was a good home for her brood, and they took over. The porch then became littered with remains of their meals (crawfish and fish; mostly crawfish) and their droppings. On rare visits when we took friends to the camp, we did not upset their routine to any extent. The family would take to the water, the young ones swimming playfully around the porch and momma, as usual, fussing from a distance. When we departed, they would again lay claim to the porch.

With winter coming on, the family split up and only lone otters would be seen. Even then, when I spotted otters and whistled, some would disappear while others reacted as though they recognized me.

Other camps with more activity did not have the advantages of our camp. Nevertheless, they often provided excellent close-up contact with local wildlife. Most every camp had a resident yellow rat snake, considered a pet by regulars but not too well accepted by visitors. Totally harmless, the snakes sometimes created a little excitement by crawling or falling on some sleeping inhabitants.

All camps had names. If an appropriate name had not been chosen, the camp was named for the person most responsible for its existence. I have forgotten many but do remember the Sugar Shack, Gator Den, Two Story, Fortenberry's, Wynett's, and Lloyd's. And, of course, there were floating houseboats that served as camps.

Camps were constructed on state property. Their builders had no legal right to do so and were, you might say, squatters. Of course, the feeling among builders and users was that the camps' existence did no harm and was actually beneficial since they provided shelter during emergencies. For quite some time, this viewpoint was shared by whichever state agency had jurisdiction.

Ranchers did not like the presence of camps, which was understandable. They had exclusive rights to hunting on their own property and felt those hunting the narrow strips of state land were harvesting their game. Also, camps sometimes housed hunters who, as we termed it at the time, "crossed the line" to hunt on private property. Ranchers were known to assemble noisy machinery on the first day of hunting season to drive game off state property onto their property.

Occasionally, fires reduced camps to ashes. Lloyd Henderson spent considerable time, effort, and more than a little money building a rather nice camp on Bulldozer Canal. After several weeks of hauling materials and doing construction, Lloyd announced one evening, "The camp is finally finished." The next day, several of us made the fifteen-mile boat journey to view the smoldering ashes.

The Two Story, also on Bulldozer, was large and, as I recall, had a porch with a wonderful view from the second floor. I believe the Two Story lasted about a month before becoming ashes. Some of us watched Wynett's camp burn from the second floor of a building at Patrick Air Force Base. Although there was quite a distance between the two locations, it was an extremely clear day and the rising column of black smoke was very obvious.

There was absolutely no reason to burn our little camp. Quite some distance from any ranchland, it never housed any hunters. It was seldom used and then only to observe wildlife. The camp was certainly hard to find and maybe the arsonists, after searching for some time, spitefully burned it simply to show they had found it. It was no great loss, but after these many years resentment remains. I played detective long enough to satisfy myself who the culprits were. I may still find an opportunity to get even.

Well, that's the way it went in the old days. More recently, it's been decided time and again that the camps must go, always for the same two reasons: the camps are eyesores and have no sewage facilities! As for being eyesores, I disagree. Visitors love to take pictures of the camps and consider them rustic. An eyesore would be something sleek and modernistic perched out there amid natural surroundings. As for sewage facilities, as the number of people using the area constantly multiplies, perhaps the decision makers have plans for a network of Porta-Potties out there in the marsh.

As I write this, I am aware of only two camps and two houseboats remaining. Perhaps tomorrow they too will be gone.

Nicknames and Explanations

OVER THE YEARS WE HAVE FOUND that nicknames are not only helpful, they are in fact essential. Each nickname allows for instant identification—a quality that is obviously lacking with the use of common names. It would be well for the entire nation to adopt our technique, but then some unsavory characters might object if they were called Loan Shark Joe, Thievin' Willie, Dishonest Dan, Shyster Sam, or some other handle.

Imagine having four regulars called Bob and someone mentions that Bob caught a big turtle. Confusion reigns and needless conversation goes on and on to determine which Bob caught the turtle. It is so much simpler when someone says, "Golfin' Bob caught a big turtle." Then we can go on to other things like, "How much did it weigh?" or "What did he catch it on?"

We have had Golfin' Bob, Fuzzy Faced Bob, Big Bob, Hog Head Bob, Neighbor Bob, and probably others I have forgotten. We once had a problem with Charlie but this was easily solved when the original Charlie retained his title and the newcomer became New York Charlie. Incidentally, when New York Charlie decided to live in Florida year-round instead of only coming down for the winter, Ralph classified him as a leftover tourist. John worked at the water plant so he became Water Plant John. No problem at all until the water plant complicated things by hiring another John. The newcomer, however, soon became White Water Plant John and things returned to normal.

Another time there were two Ernies. One was a big old boy, so quite naturally they became Big Ernie and Little Ernie. Big

Ernie was truly big, but Little Ernie was not little and resented the moniker. The problem was solved by keeping the name Big Ernie and allowing Little Ernie to become, once again, just Ernie.

Hardly anyone could remember what Abe Lincoln's real name was, but he looked like Abe Lincoln so Dick assigned him that title. He will probably never become president, but he is a fine fellow.

Sometimes the nicknames didn't seem to make sense. Take Atlanta Al for instance. He wasn't from Atlanta and his name wasn't Al. His name was actually Roy and he lived in East Point. Roy would come down from Georgia quite often and could always find time to visit with the fish camp crowd. He was a very good pool player and had played some of the best. All those other big-time pool players around the country seemed to have nicknames so it was only fitting that Roy be assigned a comparable title. We laid the handle Atlanta Al on him and it stuck. When Roy passed away, his son thoughtfully saw to it that the nickname was included in his obituary. After all, folks around these parts knew who Atlanta Al was.

There are always a bunch of Smiths and they will all be called Smitty. Now we are back to the original problem. Which Smitty? Anyway, we sorted them all out and now have Smitty, the senior Smitty, Shorty Smith, and Smitty the Barrister. We became so desperate with the Smiths that we even call one of them by his actual name, Fred.

The Old Man is an honorary title given to commanders in the service, or as in our case, to the fellow who owned the camp. We had two Steves and one of them had a pigtail, so he became Hippie Steve.

Footsie apparently earned his name when the other guys said he was shoving his foot through the carburetor, trying to get more speed from his airboat. There were so many Jacks we considered assigning numbers, but let me tell you, this won't work. Each wants to be Number 1, not Number 6.

Some other nicknames I may not have mentioned are:

Lightnin', Marsh, Buckshot, Big Jim, Radar, J.T., Dickie Doo, Pepper Pete, Bicycle Jim, Bubba, Michigan Jack, Miss Kentucky, Kinky, Jimbo, Hairlip Bill, Tally, Duke, Butch, Bud, Aggie, Zero, Earl the Pearl, Golfball Eddie, Slick, and Uncle Milty. One group, appropriately or not, is known as the Beach Boys.

Now for a few other helpful explanations:

- Kicker boats are those with an outboard motor on the back. Airboats are those with a big fan on the back.
- Everyone should know what a Georgia credit card is, but in case some don't, I will explain. It is a short piece of garden hose used to transfer fuel.
- Three jacks may beat three tens, but they sure won't beat three queens, if you know what I mean.
- Any soft drink is a soda and minnows are actually minners.
- A gator is a gator, not an alligator, and since water snakes are hard to identify, all are called moccasins.
- A borrow pit is a hole in the ground created by someone borrowing dirt with absolutely no intention of ever paying it back.
- Since the St. Johns River runs from south to north, upriver is downriver and downriver is upriver, if that makes any sense. So much for explanations.

Fishing

CONTRARY TO WHAT ONE MIGHT READ in a magazine or see on TV, fishing expeditions do not always result in a huge catch of large fish. Fishing memories are similar. While TV shows discard the unproductive film, memories of poor fishing trips simply fade away.

Extremely poor fishing should be quietly tolerated. This is not always possible. I recall one event from several years back that provided a laugh or two. A pretty large bass tournament was being held somewhere up north, and due to the advance publicity, many folks awaited the publication of results in the newspaper. The winner, it seems, caught one fish that weighed one and a half pounds. He won total weight and big bass prize. Since no other fish were caught, the remaining prizes went unclaimed. After months of promotion the sponsors would much rather the tournament be immediately forgotten.

It can and does happen. Even back when our local fishing was absolutely great, it would all but come to a halt when various conditions occurred. During the winter months, for example, a sudden cold front could give all the fish a case of lockjaw. One day you might catch all the nice-size bass you wanted, but the next day would not produce a single strike.

Floods and droughts also have a profound effect. Periods of flooding are great. Fish retreat to marshes where food is plentiful, growing fat and reproducing at an unbelievable rate. True, you don't catch many fish because they are where you can't reach them, but as I see it, this is another benefit of high water.

Droughts and low water are disastrous since we have little deep water. When the marshes dry up, the fish must retreat to the river run and the lakes. Then, if a drought persists, the southernmost lakes become nothing more than mud holes and all the fish are confined to a water surface area that is perhaps ten percent of what it should be. Food is soon exhausted, fungus infections become rampant, and it will take years for the fish to recover. Well anyway, I just wanted to explain that fishing is not always perfect. So much for that.

My first serious bass fishing trip on the St. Johns River was during January of 1966, with a rented boat and my trusty ten horsepower motor.

Fishing information was hard to come by because hardly anyone was fishing. Departing the fish camp and traveling south, all the territory looked absolutely great and I soon shut the motor off to fish. Lo and behold, about the fifth cast, a big bass inhaled the lure. It was the largest bass I had ever hooked, so you can imagine my excitement. After many runs and jumps, that rascal was in my landing net, then in the live well.

Being close to the camp and having fished only five minutes, this appeared to be an excellent opportunity to show off. Pappy was working that day as I proudly took the fish inside and asked him to weigh it. Pappy wasn't at all impressed. He put the fish on the scales, where it registered seven and a half pounds, and casually said, "Pretty nice fish, but it isn't a big one." This certainly deflated me, so I released the fish, got back in the boat, and headed out again. I caught several more fish and released them all. Some were almost as large as the first one, but Pappy had ruined my perspective of what constituted a big bass. After about three hours I hooked a true monster and was lucky enough to land it. Ready to quit fishing anyway, I put this one in the live well and returned to the camp. Ol' Pappy, still not impressed, looked at my fish and put it on the scales, which this time read nine and a half pounds. His only comment was, "That's a little better."

Pappy may not have been impressed with my fish, but his attitude certainly left an impression with me. What amazing bonanza of fishing had I stumbled on when my two largest bass ever deserved only a casual glance?

Several weeks later, when Henry, the owner of the camp, and I became friends, I told him about my first visit. Henry quit laughing long enough to say, "Pappy was giving you the business. That was the heaviest bass weighed in at the camp during the last three years."

Bass fishing back then was so good it almost defies description. I often moved away from concentrations of two- to four-pound bass in search of a lone fish of much larger size. At that time, all my fish were released on the spot. Pappy's mistreatment on that first trip must have had a lasting effect. I no longer brought fish in to show them off. Henry always inquired about my fishing success but no doubt placed little credibility in my fish stories since he never saw any fish.

All this changed some few months later when my old buddy Dave moved to this part of the country. Dave wanted to keep what we caught, so as a result there was normally a bragging-sized stringer at the end of each day's fishing. Finally, Henry could start believing my fishing accounts.

Our bass fishing was probably the best in the state at the time and few people knew about it. There had been seven years of consistently high water, so the bass were big and plentiful. If I hadn't been here to observe, like many others I would find some of the stories a bit difficult to believe.

There were no bass clubs, no bass boats, and no bass tournaments. Most of the time you wouldn't even see another fisherman.

"Caught my limit."

"Ten bass?"

"Heck no. MY limit. A little turtle and one small catfish."

There was the time I took a blind man fishing. To be perfectly honest, he wasn't really blind, he just couldn't see.

My buddy J.T. had recently had an eye operation, was wearing very dark glasses, and could hardly see anything. He couldn't work and was just killing time until things returned to normal.

When I suggested that J.T. join me on a brief fishing trip to Sawgrass, he was reluctant but eventually agreed to go when I explained there was nothing to it. I knew where the fish were and all that was required was to throw a lure in their general direction. I also knew precisely where to find a seven-pound bass.

To make a long story short, I would simply tell J.T. to cast straight ahead, to his left, or to his right. And we caught fish. The climax came when I put him on the big one. He hooked and fought it for quite some time, but since he was unable to see the obstructions, the fish escaped into a mass of vegetation.

With his eyesight repaired, J.T. can now see as well as most folks and can again fish with the best of them.

A monster in Sawgrass? That may be over doing it a little, so let's call it a USO—an unidentified swimming object. It was one of those unexplained fishing mysteries that will never be solved.

Casting for bass along the north end of Lake Sawgrass, I hooked something that offered no reaction to being hooked. I sat there dumbfounded while my twelve pound line slowly peeled off the reel. After some time it became obvious that twelve pounds of pressure was doing nothing to alter the direction or speed of whatever it was on the end of the line. There was no choice but to crank up the motor and follow. After retrieving some hundred yards of fishing line, I moved the boat off to the side, thinking pressure from that direction might change its course. Nothing. The creature continued in a perfectly straight line at the same relatively slow speed.

This continued as we crossed the lake. I would pull from one side then the other, trying to get some reaction all with no results. As we neared the south entrance to Lake Sawgrass I had been trailing that thing for nearly one and a half miles, while its direction and speed had not changed in the slightest and the creature had not shown itself. Had all this occurred in the ocean, it would have been reasonable to assume I had snagged a slow-moving submarine.

I would have followed that thing all day just for a glimpse, but as we neared the opening, the lure simply came loose. A bass? Most certainly not, it didn't fight like one. A huge catfish? Doubtful, although catfish in the area might reach forty pounds. I would have turned a forty-pound catfish in that distance. How about a mammoth turtle? There were, and still are, some big turtles in the vicinity, but none that large. Perhaps a gator? That is about the only thing left that could mistreat me in such a manner. But would a large gator go the length of Sawgrass at a constant pace, never veering left or right, maintaining the same depth, and never showing itself? Seems very doubtful, so it will remain a mystery.

Several years back, when bass fishing was incredible, I developed a routine designed to impress tourists, strangers, and sometimes even locals. Bass fishing at the time was so predictable my routine was nearly always successful.

On days when fishing conditions were absolutely perfect I would visit with Henry for a short while, then mention, for the benefit of those in the camp, that I was going fishing and would be back in about thirty minutes with a big bass. My definition of a big bass, at the time, was one of six pounds or more. The tourists would normally quiz Henry about my prognostication and Henry would simply say, "He does it all the time. Stick around and see for yourself."

Like I say, it nearly always worked.

One of those thirty-minute fishing trips produced such amazing results, it will never be forgotten.

There was a pretty young lady fishing off the old wooden bridge. She looked like she was about twenty or twenty-one and this was her second day on the bridge. Someone would bring her out in the morning and she fished all day. Then, in the late afternoon, they came back to pick her up. She just fished and never came in the camp. Seemed friendly enough and always spoke, but had probably been told to stay away from the nasty fish camp crowd.

Well, anyway, this time I came in with a bass over nine pounds that I removed from the live well and carried inside to weigh. The little ole girl got pretty excited about my fish, but still didn't come down off the bridge. After weighing the fish and answering the customary questions, I returned the fish to the river. All of a sudden, I was really getting cussed out! That cute little girl was using some words I surely hadn't expected. Her final statement was, "If my daddy was here you wouldn't throw that *&%$#@ fish back!"

It was a darn shame. Had I known she wanted the fish, I would have given it to her.

The Sheriff

IT MAY HAVE APPEARED that pulling harmless pranks on visitors was a favorite fish camp pastime. In all fairness, most of the situations were set up by the visitors themselves. Oftentimes the opportunities were in fact irresistible.

Back when the Space Program was the foremost local tourist attraction, Henry, on many occasions, put me in an embarrassing position with one of his pranks. My job was remoteely associated, but Henry, not satisfied with my lowly position, elevated me to the top. Whenever strangers wanted to discuss the Space Program, Henry would startle them with, "Jack over there is the guy that pushes the button. If he doesn't push the button, the launch doesn't go!" It happened so often that I became adept at deflecting questions and employed that famous stopper, "We can't talk about that subject, it's classified." As ridiculous as it might seem, these tourists wanted to believe Henry so they could carry tales back home of having met the man who pushed the button.

As we shall see, "the sheriff" was one of Henry's better efforts. It was a Sunday afternoon and I had been fishing. I was now parked in my favorite chair in the far corner of the camp, having a beer before going home. It was one of those days where there was practically no activity around the camp. Henry and I were the only people present when a car pulled off the highway, parked, and six very obviously Yankee tourists crawled out to slowly file into the camp.

The group had come from the west, Osceola County—no

Sunday beer sales. Now the county line is but a short distance away, but Brevard County does allow purchase of beer on Sunday.

Once inside these folks aimlessly walked around looking at the photographs, gator skulls, snake skins, all the other oddities, and apparently my can of beer.

It was some time before one of the fellows eased up to Henry and whispered, "Can we get a beer?" Henry, with the situation well figured out, whispered back, "I guess I could let you have a round."

The group seated themselves around a table and very quietly sipped their beer. It had probably been an extremely hot, dry ride through Osceola County. After awhile one of them returned to the bar and whispered a request for a second round. Henry opened six beers, spoke a few words that I couldn't hear, and the gentleman carried the beers to their table. The mood changed as the strangers became very talkative, and one by one each came by to visit and chat with me. After another round and lots more conversation they were ready to leave. They thanked Henry for the beer, and on their way out stopped to say how glad they were to have met me.

When they had cleared out and it was back to just the two of us, I asked Henry, "What did you tell those people?" Henry said, "I told them you were the sheriff of this county and as long as the damned sheriff could sit here and drink beer on Sunday, I would serve them all they wanted.

I wonder what wild vacation yarns this little encounter prompted when the visitors returned home.

So I had been a successful button pusher and sheriff, what next?

We were visiting Henry and Ruby at their new home outside

Ocala where they had moved after selling the camp. Since I was not at all familiar with the area, Henry took me for a tour that included stops at two of the local establishments. The first stop was quite normal. We had a beer, visited with the folks, and moved on. Thanks to Henry though, the second stop proved to be anything but normal.

This was a large place with twenty-five or thirty customers, apparently retirees since it was early afternoon on a weekday. I made a visit to the restroom and when I returned everyone started calling me Charlie. Then one by one they all came by to tell me fishing stories. One told of catching a twenty-eight pound bass, and some of the stories—though not logical—were very interesting.

None of this made much sense to me until one of the fellows said, "Will you make sure that gets in the paper?" Now I began to smell a rat. I asked Henry, "What did you tell these guys?" Henry replied, "I told them you were Charlie," who was a well-known fishing and hunting writer for the Orlando newspaper.

Well, so as not to mess up such a well-laid scheme, I got out a small notepad and pen and started recording some of these unusual events. It wasn't long before my little notepad was full of unofficial world record fishing information and we couldn't even buy a beer. I certainly hope those folks are not still waiting for their accounts to be published in the paper.

Blow Boats

YOU MAY SOMETIMES HEAR AIRBOATS REFERRED TO as blow boats. Of course, you may also hear them called other names, less complimentary and maybe even vulgar. But that's OK. Airboats still have their place, and if manatees had any say in the matter, all boats would be airboats.

Logically, the name blow boat is more appropriate than airboat. This craft is not meant to become airborne. When one does, as occasionally happens, the operator may find himself in a world of hurt. Blowers they are, and they put those little, sissy, hand-held, noisy leaf blowers to shame.

Tourists can always be counted on to provide loads of entertainment when they're experiencing their first close-up look at airboats in action. You will normally find the average tourist decked out in sunglasses and a large straw hat as protection against our fierce Florida sun. And he'll be carrying an expensive camera. He'll invariably maneuver into position for an exciting close-up shot just as the boat reaches the water and the operator showers down on the gas pedal. Results? The tourist and camera receive an unexpected shower, the sunglasses may be retrieved from their landing place one hundred feet away, and the straw hat sails majestically far out into the marsh, never to be seen again!

This is not a good time to ask the tourist his favorite name for airboats.

Sometimes the combination of a blow boat and a camera can unexpectedly produce an award-winning home video. The water level was above normal when Julio decided to explore some remote reaches with his son-in-law on the bow, video camera in hand, capturing on film this wild and beautiful locale with all its seldom disturbed wildlife.

Whoops! An unexpected sandbar just below the surface! Quite naturally, the boat stopped but the son-in-law didn't! Overboard into the underboard! This would have been accepted as a normal, routine blow boat experience had not the camera kept rolling. There on film is the boat with some startled-looking occupants, the beautiful blue sky, a glimpse of the surrounding marshland, and a bit of spray and mud from impact. Absolutely no harm done. The camera could be wiped off and the clothing dumped into the washer. Recorded for posterity was one more episode in the life of Julio LaMuck, airboater extraordinaire.

Some may remember H&H Airboats, an enterprise started by Bobby Hopwood and Lloyd Henderson. Lloyd didn't hang with it for long, but Bobby continued, building a few boats, maintaining a stock of parts, and providing repairs. It was a rather excited Bobby who showed up at the camp one morning with news that he had a contraption that would most certainly revolutionize marsh fishing hereabouts—a small engine with prop and guard, which, when clamped onto the transom of a jon boat, converted it to an airboat. With no underwater propeller, fishermen would be able to skim through the marsh and reach those choice locations no one had ever fished. When this device caught on, Bobby wouldn't be able to keep them in stock and would have an exclusive franchise for the entire Southeast.

All activity ceased as everyone watched Bobby launch a large aluminum jon boat and mount the lightweight apparatus. Quite frankly, it looked like a large office fan. It started on the first pull and Bobby was off. Or was he? The boat moved but just barely. Bobby nosed the rig back onto the bank and announced that the boat was simply too large and he would get a smaller one. Bobby departed to search for a smaller boat, and fish camp conversation returned to important subjects, such as how many points Alabama would score against Florida in the upcoming Saturday football game. As usual, there was no question that Alabama would win; the question was how badly would Florida be beaten. (I might add that this was B.S.: Before Spurrier.)

Not gone for long, Bobby reappeared with a twelve-foot aluminum jon boat. Quite frankly, no one should venture out in anything smaller unless he or she is an Olympic swimmer. No problem since the entire rig weighed next to nothing. Now Bobby fired up and headed across the river. With a slight breeze at his back, Bobby moved along but seemed to have only three speeds: slow, slower, and stopped. In due time he proceeded under the bridge and out of sight up the canal alongside old 192. Not overly impressed by the demonstration thus far, the critics returned to the camp.

We continued to hear the motor, but the sound seemed to come from one location, as though the boat wasn't moving. About one beer later we could see the boat, and it sure wasn't breaking any speed records. That slight breeze that had been at Bobby's back was now in his face. The boat's speed? Well, let's just say he should have taken his lunch and a six pack. He could have made much better time with a paddle but had neglected to take one with him. I'm sure someone could have taken his own boat out to tow Bobby in, but that would have spoiled the fun. Everyone yelled suggestions and comments, which Bobby couldn't hear or chose to ignore as he tacked back and forth like he was on a sailboat. He seemed to gain maybe a foot with each of these tacking maneuvers, and, friends, the river is several feet wide at this point. The motor droned on and the observers again lost interest. Bobby was on his own.

A number of beers and perhaps three hours had expired when the motor stopped running. Bobby had made it back to the launch ramp. Normally, someone would have helped him load the boat. Not on this occasion, however. Best to just let him cool down a little. With the boat loaded and ready to go, Bobby came into the camp and someone bought him a beer. There was no mention of the fiasco, which was just as well considering all his buddies had left him out there unaided in the hot sun. And what happened with that exclusive franchise and Bobby's expectations of making a bundle? Can't really say since this was the only time we ever saw one of those contraptions in use.

Many blow boat accomplishments and perhaps some failures resulted from a sequence of events that followed a pattern. If there was a recipe for such adventures and misadventures, it consisted of only two ingredients: a plentiful supply of beer and a group of blow boaters.

Danny, Richard, and some of the others had been out in their boats, had visited some of the hard-to-reach places, had burned considerable gas, and now, with their boats silenced, simply lounged around on the lake shore near the launch ramp. There was beer left from their ride, and if they ran out it was only a short walk to the fish camp and an inexhaustible supply.

Conversation, of course, covered many subjects but seemed to inevitably return to blow boats and what they could or could not do. Danny's boat, when it was running, ran well. Oh, he might abuse it a little sometimes, but, unlike many, he always put it back into A-1 condition before going out again.

The subject turned to running dry—without water, that is—and, bear in mind, this was before polymer, that slick material now applied to boat bottoms. Everyone knew Danny's boat ran dry exceptionally well, but maybe he was overdoing it when he said he could run to the water plant and back—not a great distance if you were driving a car, riding a horse, or peddling a bicycle. Offhand, I'd say it's about a quarter mile each way. Someone, probably thinking Danny would back down, offered to bet $100 it couldn't be done. You might say he didn't know Danny very well. Without a whole bunch of conversation, Danny accepted the bet, crawled onto his boat and fired it up. The ramp was clear and the road was clear as Danny made a turn on the lake and hit the launch ramp at full throttle. Up the ramp he went, then on down the blacktop road at a pretty good speed. Everyone got into a position to watch as he continued without slowing. He was temporarily out of sight when he made the loop through the water plant driveway, but you could hear the gravel flying. Back on the blacktop and headed back for the ramp, he hadn't slowed a bit. Jane, who had come out of the fish camp to raise a fuss about all the commotion, very nearly got run over and had to scramble out of Danny's path.

Yes, sir, he had made the round trip with ease and now went back down the ramp and into the lake for what could be called a victory lap. A slight problem now became apparent, though, as water came up through the bottom of the boat like a geyser, shooting maybe twenty feet into the air. Danny took his shower in stride and eased the boat back up the bank just as it was about to go to the bottom.

We'll not get into the cost of a new hull and all that. Danny won the bet!

Airboaters

IF ONE GROUP HAS CONTRIBUTED MORE than any other to fish camp lore, it would be, hands down, the airboaters. They have come a long ways with their present-day large, sophisticated engines, big stable hulls, and polymer bottoms. And, for better or for worse, they have multiplied. It is not at all like it was years back when airboats were so few you could recognize from the sound of the engine which boat was running a mile away in the marsh. Most did not have starters, so hand propping and busted knuckles were a way of life. Some didn't even have prop guards, which was downright foolish, but even with a guard, foreign objects often found a way through to destroy a perfectly good, expensive prop.

Billy's 65 HP engine would not start when it was hot. People offered advice and many worked on the engine, but a cure was never found. It simply would not start when hot. His only option, therefore, was to make certain the engine was not shut off until he reached his destination. Following that, a two-hour cooling-off period was necessary before going elsewhere. So, what happened when Billy accidentally killed the engine two hundred yards from the camp in a clump of willows? Two full hours out in the hot grueling sun with not one sign of a breeze. We couldn't get close enough to pull the boat out, but Jeff did wade the marsh to deliver a cold beer to Billy and Bob. Appreciated? Well, after twenty-some years, the two beers are still being repaid.

In regard to sinking, George insists, and understandably so, that all airboaters can be classified in one of two groups: 1) those who have and 2) those who will.

Airboat sinkings were a common occurrence, but remember, many of these boats were quite small. If someone so much as stood on the corner of a transom the boat might go under. Hank learned this the hard way while trying to be helpful.

Following a toad strangler of a rain some of us went outside where Hank noticed this airboat nearly full of water. Good guy that he was, he found a bucket and, without asking anyone's advice, decided to bail the boat. One single step from the bank to the boat's transom was all it took. Down went the boat, Hank, and the bucket. It was funny for an instant, but there is a great deal of difference between bailing a boat and raising one from the bottom of a canal.

The two airboaters, wanting no more of Hank's help, slightly hinted at physical violence if he were even to watch the recovery operation. Surely Radar didn't sink every time out. He must have made a few successful roundtrips that we simply don't remember. Regardless of all that, whenever he fired up his boat and roared off the bank, the same question was always asked, "Who is going after him this time?"

The individual record for quite some time was three sinkings in one day. That was surpassed in about 1976 when Footsie sold his little nine footer and the new owner managed to sink four times the first morning he ran it. Three times in shallow water where, with volunteer help, he could get it up, dried out, and running again. The fourth sinking occurred in deeper water and he was done for the day. That record still stands, but imagine what it might have been had he remained in shallow water.

We were fishing a bend in the river. It was one of those days when nobody else was out—we hadn't seen another boat until an airboat could be heard approaching from the south. It was Irvin on a boat he had just finished assembling. A shakedown cruise no doubt, but the end result was Irvin being shaken up. When he drew even with us we waved and he waved back. As luck would have it, at that very instant, the steering linkage broke and Irvin was off through the willows. With no brakes or reverse he went pretty deep into the brush before getting stopped. We couldn't get close enough to see him but a shout brought the reply, "No problem, everything is okay." With a temporary repair job, he got the boat squared away and came back out of the willows, nothing damaged except his pride and reputation.

Another time, as Irvin put his boat in the water Jeff took up a position on the old bridge. After quite some time we became curious and yelled, "What are you doing?" Jeff replied, "Keeping an eye on Irvin so I will know where to go get him when he breaks down." Sure enough, a few minutes later Jeff came down off the bridge and left in the kicker boat. Another thirty minutes and he was coming back, towing Irvin and his disabled boat.

Good Ole Irvin didn't have a monopoly on bad luck but he definitely had his fair share. Bobby always said that someday he would invent training wheels for new airboaters, but I guess he never perfected the design.

Others may be a bit dubious but all airboaters readily accept the next incident. This fellow, finished running for the day, loaded his boat on the trailer only to find that his truck wouldn't start. After some unsuccessful tinkering he arrived at a solution. With a piece of fishing line rigged to the gas pedal on the airboat and passed through the truck window, he simply fired off the boat's engine and pushed the truck home. It was too bad that a state patrolman gave him a ticket for not going the minimum speed on I-95.

With the river extremely high, marshes flooded and ditches filled, there wasn't enough clearance for airboats to get under the bridge. All the airboaters took to jumping over the road since they couldn't get under the bridge, and this developed into a new sport—racing airboats against automobiles. Just imagine yourself as a tourist cruising down 192, when suddenly you hear an aircraft engine and glance out the side window to see you are being overtaken by an airboat buzzing along in the ditch. Usually the boat won, but that might be attributed to the surprise factor.

I was sitting on the porch visiting with a tourist and Bobby was running west in the ditch. The tourist, this being his first encounter with airboats asked, "Where is he going?" An excellent opportunity for a touch of in-camp humor. I told him Bobby was a little low on gas so he was running to the service station at Holopaw. The tourist asked, "That's a little far, isn't it?" I answered, "Yes, but as fast as Bobby goes he will be back in a few minutes." Well this fellow got himself another beer and sat back down awaiting Bobby's return. Just as I had said, about twenty minutes later, here came Bobby roaring down the ditch from the opposite direction. After parking his boat he came inside and I asked, "Was the station open when you got to Holopaw?" Sensing the put-on, Bobby replied, "Sure, they are always open, I filled the tank."

The visitor, now satisfied that airboats were incredible, finished his beer and said "So long," as he headed back to the beach. What a story he would have to tell his fellow tourists.

We will return to the subject of airboats, that is inevitable, but for now, let's move on to other things.

Marsh Fires

THEY MAY NOT RANK AMONG the premier attractions of Florida, but be assured, marsh fires can be quite spectacular. When hundreds, sometimes thousands of acres of marsh are burning, it is certainly impressive and particularly so during darkness. At times the entire horizon appears to be burning. We do not have exclusive rights to marsh fires, but with many miles of St. Johns River marsh nearby, it is safe to say we have our fair share.

Occurring primarily during winter or early spring, the fires cause surprisingly little damage, and in many respects, may actually prove to be beneficial. There is, however, the ever-present possibility of a marsh fire becoming a muck fire and, for sure, nothing at all good can be said for a muck fire.

The marshes contain a layer of peat, which may vary from a few inches to several feet in thickness. And peat, being a natural fuel, will certainly burn when dry.

Why is it that when the peat starts burning it is called a muck fire? Muck is generally considered to be wet, soggy, and muddy. There is no evident answer to this question, so since the term has been used for generations, let's accept it. When the peat starts burning, it is a muck fire.

Muck fires are the culprits that can shut down highways, cause respiratory problems, and create multi-vehicle chain reaction accident. So, again, nothing good can be said for muck fires.

What causes marsh fires? The usual answer to this question is lightning. Even though no lightning has been sighted for a week, Mother Nature is to blame. One might wonder, at times, if

Mother Nature may have received a tiny bit of help from a rancher, hunter, or some other well-meaning individual.

Charlie, living on a houseboat near the bridge, was having trouble with the varmints. No big deal—it kind of came with the territory since his boat was tied up next to the marsh and the makeshift wooden walkway was sometimes underwater. Frost had thoroughly burned the marsh vegetation so that it was now brown and dry, and with a slight breeze from the east, conditions couldn't be better. If he burned the marsh, it would not dispose of the snakes, rats, and all the rest, but it would eliminate the dense, matted cover and those varmints would have to find somewhere else to live. It shouldn't cause any problems—with the east wind it would burn that relatively small area of marsh then peter out when it reached the fringes. So much for good intentions.

Charlie fired off the dry material alongside his houseboat and watched for a while until satisfied that everything was going according to plan. He soon lost interest, however, and retired to the boat for a nap. No one else paid much attention—it was simply a harmless little marsh fire. Awaking sometime later, Charlie, from the porch, admired his handiwork. Where there had been dense, tangled marsh growth five and six feet high, there was now nothing but blackened ashes. Little remained of the fire itself, just smoldering isolated patches where the growth had been unusually thick or perhaps a little damp. The wind had shifted somewhat, but that by now was of no consequence.

Something caught Charlie's attention. Due to the wind change, the tinder dry material on the road embankment had unexpectedly burned! That's where his car was parked!

From a distance, as he hurried across the walkway, the car appeared to be unharmed. But was it? Afraid not. Close examination revealed that both front tires were virtually melted. There was no other damage since there was no flammable material near the rest of the automobile, but Charlie's nap had cost him two tires.

Next year, when it came time to burn the marsh, Charlie would make certain his car was parked in a safer location.

Curious about the effects of a marsh fire on local wildlife, I quit fishing to watch as a fire approached from the west. Driven by a moderate breeze, it was no raging inferno, but from a distance was very impressive. Several hundred acres were involved.

First came the rabbits, rats, and mice scurrying ahead of the flames. They were in danger of course, but gave no appearance of panic. Each of these animals, as far as I could determine, found a secure, fireproof haven along the edge of the river. They would probably have swum to the other side had it become necessary.

Next came the birds—all sorts of birds, representing every species in the vicinity. They leapfrogged ahead of the flames, feeding on the countless insects. As the flames neared the river, thousands of those insects started falling in the water and it was absolutely unbelievable, the number of fish which began feeding. Apparently, through some sort of communication, fish were drawn from up and down the river to this bonanza of floating, kicking insects. Big fish, little fish. As with the birds, it seemed every species was represented. The feeding frenzy continued even after the fire reached the river's edge and the insects stopped falling. When the fish eventually stopped breaking water, not a single insect remained on the surface.

There were stretches of the river the fire had not yet reached, so I chose another observation location and was treated to a second demonstration equaling the first. It appeared the birds and fish, like myself, moved from one area to another, wherever the insects were most abundant.

This particular fire ignited some deposits of peat, which burned for several days. Not a full-fledged muck fire, but nonetheless, a muck fire. Some weeks later, when the marsh had regained most of its greenery, I tied the boat to a willow for a short walk through the spongy peat moss. From such a minor fire, there were holes that had burned to a depth of five feet. A very treacherous area for a stroll.

Another memorable marsh fire from several years back did virtually no damage, but kept a crew of volunteer firemen occupied for quite some time and, through the efforts of one fish camp resident, created a great deal of temporary public interest.

This was a full-fledged marsh fire with hundreds of acres burning on both sides of the highway. During daylight it had not been too impressive, but when darkness descended, with miles of marsh burnings and the entire western skyline lit up, it certainly caught the attention of folks in town.

Nothing was actually in serious danger. The fish camp with its cabins was uncomfortably close to the inferno, prompting the local fire department to bring equipment to the scene, but barring a severe wind change, the buildings were in little jeopardy.

Living in one of the cabins at the time was a gentleman, name long since forgotten, who worked at a local radio station. This fellow, among other things, was a very accomplished jokester. The fire situation, as he saw it, was an excellent opportunity simply going to waste.

Calling Henry aside, our unnamed friend has a proposition. "You know, you only have three customers. How would you like to fill the place up?"

Henry, totally confused and not knowing what to expect, replied, "Sure, why not?"

With that, the radioman made a brief call to his station to be hooked up for a special service announcement:

"Your attention please! There is a very serious fire in the marsh along side Route 192 at the St. Johns River! The fish camp is in danger, but firefighters and equipment are on the scene doing their best to contain the inferno! It is requested that the public refrain from visiting this area since congestion might hinder the efforts of the firefighters! Thank you, we shall now return to the music in progress."

Human nature being what it is, within fifteen minutes the parking area was filled with cars and Henry needed assistance with the beer tending. Further proof that marsh fires can be beneficial.

That Tree is About 150 Yards

AT THE TIME, SOME OF THE FISH CAMP FOLKS, myself not included, were becoming rather prosperous. This made little difference at the camp, where each person was treated for who he was, not what he possessed. However, all this prosperity, plus the simple fact that some people will bet on anything, contributed generously to the following incident. The main characters were Bob and Bobby, and, for some reason, I was designated as judge.

It was one of those late fall days with most everyone at work and only a few of us gathered at the camp. With hunting season coming on, that quite naturally became the main subject of conversation. Each participant politely took turns recounting past accomplishments that, perhaps with age, had become a bit exaggerated. The usual things—downing three ducks with one shot, bagging a deer on a dead run at two hundred yards through dense cover, hitting a large tom turkey at seventy-five yards on the fly, etc. It went on and on. If the first gentleman killed three ducks with one shot, quite naturally, the next storyteller claimed at least four. When we reached the point where Herb fired both barrels of his shotgun and totaled forty coots, it was time to change the subject.

Someone mentioned the difficulty of estimating the distance to a target. Now most people can't judge distance worth a hoot, but that ability plays a very important part in hunting success. There followed an offering of various methods for estimating distance. Some were reasonable and others downright ridiculous. No problem with that unless you couldn't recognize the difference. Bob, the only serious hunter in the group, hadn't had much to say up to now. He pointed across the river to a cabbage tree and casually remarked, "That tree is about a hundred and fifty yards." Whether Bobby could estimate distance or not, we will never know, but he immediately replied, "There ain't no way, that's only about a hundred yards!"

Now the action started. Bob asked, "You want to bet?"

Bobby said, "Sure, how much?" Now Bobby, at the time, carried a thousand dollar bill for just such emergencies. He whipped his big bill out, threw it on the table, and said, "Let's bet a thousand!" Bob rummaged through his billfold and pockets and came up with something in the neighborhood of eight hundred dollars. He asked if he could write a check for the difference, and Bobby agreed that his check was as good as cash.

With the wager settled, we now had a slight problem. The tree was on the far side of the river, back in a marshy area, and there was no tape or other measuring device available. Furthermore, members of our little group didn't mind sitting around discussing how great they were in the outdoors, but not one wanted to get wet wading the snake-infested marsh. After much more discussion, recommendations, and rebuttals, the group decided there was no way to accurately measure the distance. Let's forget it and go on to other things. Bobby put his bill away; Bob tore his check up and crammed his money in his pocket. Since nothing had been determined, I was pretty sure more would follow.

After a while Bob casually mentioned, "I'm pretty good with a twenty-two. If someone throws a can I will hit it in the air with one shot." This sounded worthwhile to me because I would have trouble hitting a thrown can with a twelve-gauge shotgun. Bobby didn't hesitate. He jumped right on this situation and declared, "A hundred bucks says you can't." Bob quietly accepted, and with the two hundred dollars lying on the table we all went outside. Since I had been selected as the official thrower and judge, I found a can and added a little sand for weight. With everyone ready, I chucked the can as best as I could and Bob touched off a shot. Not much noise from that twenty-two and I didn't see any reaction from the can. Everyone mumbled, "He missed," as I retrieved the can. To my surprise, I found perfectly neat little holes, dead center, through both sides. The can was passed around for all to inspect, then everyone went back inside where Bob collected his two hundred dollars from the table.

Hitting a thrown can with a twenty-two rifle is no small feat, so Bobby, after thinking it over, announced, "You can't do it again!" With another two hundred dollars lying on the table, everyone returned to the scene of action. I selected another can, added the appropriate amount of sand and let fly. Bob fired the little twenty-two and, once again, there was no indication that he had a hit. Regardless, when I picked it up, this can also had a neat hole through both sides. As before, Bob cleared the table of the two hundred dollars, but this time he bought everyone a beer. Then he announced, "I can hit the can twice before it touches the ground." Bobby, now minus two hundred dollars, wisely declined.

It is a matter of opinion, but for what it's worth, Bob would have hit the can twice, and that tree was almost exactly one hundred and fifty yards away.

Some folks feel that the only requirement for becoming a great hunter is enough dollars to buy a gun. Sorry to say, this also holds true with some boaters, but let's not get into that.

I remember one time this young man wanted to sight in a new rifle. He paced off about a hundred and fifty yards and hung his target on a tree, then returned and fired one round. Examination of the target revealed he had hit the paper, not the bulls eye mind you, just the target. He fired a second round from the same location and once again checked the target. There was only one hole. He was heading back to his car to put the rifle away when someone asked, "Aren't you going to shoot any more?" His reply was, "Heck no, the rifle is shooting perfectly, both bullets went through the same hole."

This young fellow had much to learn about shooting a rifle.

You are never too old to learn, and perhaps that good old boy who never has much to say could be your teacher.

Don and Bob had a little shooting match several years back—a whole bunch of discussion Saturday evening and the contest scheduled for Sunday morning. In this instance it was 30-06 versus .270. I arrived a bit late and it was all over.

We had known Bob for years but he'd never mentioned that he'd once traveled as an exhibition shooter for a major arms manufacturer. He was one of those fellows who could draw the profile of an Indian with a twenty-two rifle.

Cats

As MIGHT BE EXPECTED, cats provide an excellent subject for fish camp conversation. Whenever a few old timers are in attendance and this subject is mentioned, two or three hours of unusual stories will normally follow.

For more than two years, Whitie, the fish camp cat, had used the roof of the storage shed as his own private resting place. He could lie up there and survey the entire area or sleep to his heart's content, completely out of harm's way where nothing could disturb him. That is, until one day when Larry fired off his airboat right next to the building and everything was blown away, including the cat and some roofing. Whitie sailed about forty feet with his legs outstretched, looking like a huge white flying squirrel, before landing.

The flight didn't hurt him in the slightest, but he never again returned to the shed roof.

I haven't seen a Florida Panther in several years, and with all the development in the area they may be gone for good.

I certainly hope that somehow the panther does survive in the wild, but the situation at this time looks very bleak. Anyway, I have had two personal encounters with panthers during my relatively brief residence in the area. Not bad considering many people have lived hereabouts for their entire lives without seeing one.

About 1968, a panther moved in the area north of Route 192 and east of the river. Many people saw the cat as it crossed the highway, always at the same location. He would travel from north to south in the late evening after dark, and from south to north in the early morning before daylight. As near as could be determined this was a daily routine. Apparently the cat went hunting each night in the area south of 192, then returned early each morning to bed down for the day at some unknown location north of 192.

We saw him one evening on his way south, and Henry, since he went to town early each morning for the newspaper and a cup of coffee, saw the cat on numerous occasions. Other people often reported seeing the panther, but thankfully no big deal was made of it. He would probably have been easy pickings for anyone intent on illegally bagging a Florida Panther. About the time we were becoming accustomed to the cat, we had some very high water that probably flooded his daytime resting place. With his daily-used trail under two and three feet of water, he apparently moved to higher ground and reports of sightings ceased.

The last time I was privileged to see a Florida Panther in the wild was in 1979. Earl and I had been fishing Lake Sawgrass and decided to take a break, find some shade, and eat our snacks. The nearest shade was the Australian pines on Avocado Island at the east end of the old railroad trestle. Avocado is not actually an island, but it is an interesting, pleasant place to visit. The trail from Sawgrass is a very tight fit for a kicker boat—only a small ditch with little depth so you quietly idle through it and tie up to one of the trees.

We had walked only a short distance when suddenly a large animal bolted out of the bushes. The cover was dense and we only saw it for an instant, but there was no question that it was a young panther. Examining the sand nearby, we found numerous tracks and the spot where it had been bedded down.

This particular cat had certainly adapted to disturbance

from humans. No less than six airboats had passed within fifty feet of it that morning and we were only twenty feet away when it took off. Later, on two occasions, we found tracks at the same location, but never again saw the cat.

A few months prior to this sighting Red Bird had seen a mother panther with two small, spotted, long-tailed kittens only about ten miles away, so we guessed our panther was one of the young ones, now out on his own.

There were continued reports of a panther in the vicinity of Avocado Island. One couple who camped out claimed the cat screamed all night so they slept with a gun at their side. After about a year there were no more reports and evidently, no panther.

On one of my regular visits to the camp, Cas had the donation jar on the bar with a poster, "HELP GET HENRY OUT OF JAIL." I didn't want to be the first dummy to ask the obvious question so I just waited. The next fellow that came in quite naturally asked, "Who is Henry?" It seems Henry, the cat, had scratched a little boy and, as a result, was now incarcerated at the local Humane Society.

Henry surely had some friends, for a few days later the arrogant feline had been bailed out and was back in familiar territory, living it up as he always had.

Catch and Release

THE CANAL ALONGSIDE ROUTE 520, just west of the river, looked like good bass fishing territory, but hardly anyone ever fished it. Curious about what the canal might hold, I parked the truck well off the highway and got out to make a few casts. In a short while I landed several bass, including one of about seven pounds, which I gave to two fellows who were passing by and stopped when they saw me fighting the fish.

I am afraid these two became a bit disillusioned. They were moving to Orlando and this was the first time either of them had been to Florida. At this point they were convinced that all you had to do to catch a seven-pound bass in these parts was pull off alongside of any handy canal and cast your plastic worm.

A few minutes after the two departed I cast into some very dense vegetation and had a tremendous strike. He didn't get hooked but that made no difference. In that thick cover I would be able to get him to strike again. He did, showering water and weeds all over the place! I missed him the second time and began thinking this must be the granddaddy of all bass from the disturbance he made. The third strike I finally hooked him, but it was some time before I could tell what I had. What a disappointment, it was a gator about five feet long.

He would take out about fifty feet of line, then I could slowly get it back. When his feet touched bottom on my side of the canal he was off again. As anyone who has hooked a five-foot gator will tell you, this can go on for some time, but I was determined to get that sucker up on the bank and retrieve my plastic worm.

Passing motorists, seeing my fishing rod bent double, started slowing down and some pulled over to the side for a better look. I was remotely aware of this, but more concentrated on landing the gator. Then there was a screeching of tires, blaring of horns, and all kinds of noise! Six cars somehow managed to get stopped, but they were pointed in all directions, in one big scrambled mess. No one was injured and no cars were damaged, but it certainly was a close call. My playing with that gator had nearly caused a disaster.

It seemed a good idea to get gone before someone had something mean to say, so I clamped down on the spool, purposely breaking the line, and quit fishing for the day.

Having learned something from this experience, I would like to offer two serious items of advice. First, do not fish alongside a busy thoroughfare. Second, if you must fish in such a place, make certain you don't hook anything.

It should come as no surprise that even birds qualify for catch and release.

This large hawk, obviously someone's attempt at falconry, appeared first on power lines near the camp where he could be seen at any time, easily identified by a leather thong hanging from one leg. As the days passed the hawk moved closer to the camp, eventually choosing the lower branches of a tree near the front door as its usual perch. Seemed it wanted to be near people and was probably expecting to be fed. Everyone tried to feed the bird, but with no success at all. It wouldn't eat what we offered and seemed to have quit hunting on its own.

I intended to catch the hawk for the purpose of turning it over to the Wildlife Sanctuary or the Fish and Game Department, but knowing at least a little something about these big birds, didn't want to attempt it without proper equipment.

While I was trying to line up a pair of long leather gauntlet gloves, a heavy towel, and the other necessities, Tex and Buddy announced there was no need for all that foolishness, they would catch the bird as is, where is.

True to their word, they did catch the hawk and later released it minus the thong. All this was darned thoughtful of the two, but in later years there was considerable debate over which one actually caught the hawk. Now since Buddy lost a couple days work, had a doctor bill to pay, and still has scars, there is no doubt in my mind who did the deed.

Celebrities

D*URING THEIR HEYDAY* the fish camps played host to a vast variety of well-known individuals. For the most part, they came to sample the fishing although some were here for airboat rides, which provided an opportunity to view the St. Johns River and marshes. Without exception, these folks were pleasant, enjoyable individuals who wanted to be treated like everyone else. They normally disliked special attention and could do without idle conversation concerning whatever accomplishments had brought them celebrity status. After all, if they wanted recognition and attention they would have gone to one of the big-time places on the beach, rather than an out-of-the-way, isolated little old fish camp.

Because of this, there was an unwritten, but well-understood, rule among the fish camp regulars. Celebrities would go unrecognized and be treated no differently than any other visitors.

Just to mention a few types—there were famous generals, college football coaches, college football players, major league baseball managers, many major league players, movie stars, TV personalities, and at least one astronaut. Incidentally, there were other notorious people whom we will omit. They did not qualify as celebrities since their fame had been gained through less than legitimate endeavors.

An early-morning party of fisherman, before starting out, wanted to make arrangements for lunch. Henry assured them a fine meal upon their return, as indeed it was. Little did they know that Henry had been unable to locate the already-prepared meal he desperately wanted to serve one member of the group. A can of leftover World War II C-rations! The big, tall, easily recognized fellow was General Mark Clark and C-rations were what Henry had survived on while serving under the general in Italy.

One of the nation's best-known, highest-paid professional football players arrived two days late. He had met this girl on his flight to New Orleans and, you might say, he had taken a two-day delay en route. Being two days behind schedule, he had time only for a brief airboat ride.

Baseball manager Billy Martin and several of his staff unexpectedly showed up for a fishing expedition. Now Billy was my favorite manager, but after getting off work by the time I reached the camp they had departed. They didn't catch many fish but had I been there to show them around, it might have been a different story.

We often wonder about the fellow who was an extremely good golfer. He showed up one day and stayed for a full week. No one ever learned his name—we called him by his nickname, Rabbit. There is reason to believe he may be one of the better-known golfers now playing on the Senior Circuit.

Back to the astronaut. Two couples that had been airboating came in the camp for a little break, probably to get relief from the hot sun and noise. The two men started a friendly game of eight ball while the ladies just relaxed. After a while, Bobby quietly passed the word that one of the pool players was an astronaut. With this tip we readily recognized him from the newspaper pictures and TV appearances. Everyone behaved as they should, without giving any indication that this fellow was anyone special, and just casually watched the pool game. I must admit, the play wasn't very impressive, but then perhaps because of all the time required for training the astronaut had become a bit rusty. Maybe he would improve after a couple of games. Not so. Game two was as bad as game one and game three was no better.

With the conclusion of game four, Henry violated the cardinal rule of the fish camp when he announced in a rather loud voice, "He may know how to get to the moon and back, but he doesn't know doodley squat about eight ball!"

Everyone in the place had a good laugh, and then things returned to normal. The pool game continued with no dumb questions or senseless conversation. The astronaut, beyond a doubt, in spite of his poor showing at pool, had become just another good old boy at the fish camp.

Land Snakes Alive!

MANY FOLKS DO NOT LIKE SNAKES, or it would probably be more appropriate to say that they are afraid of snakes. This is easily understood and appreciated but the fear is unnecessary. Fact is that snakes treat humans much better than humans treat snakes. Nonpoisonous snakes, in my opinion, should never be harmed and poisonous snakes should only be eliminated when they are in areas frequented by humans. This opinion, of course, will not be overwhelmingly endorsed, but as time goes by and the younger folks have a chance to learn, snakes will be better appreciated.

So much for that. It is unlikely that I can change anyone's opinion of snakes, but I shall keep trying.

Our entire local area must have been, at one time, an ideal habitat for a variety of snakes. Sorry to say though, snakes and gopher turtles probably suffer more from development and man's encroachment than most other native residents. Twenty some years ago I was fortunate enough to find what I considered to be the ideal home site. Two plus acres out in the boondocks, no houses, no people, no problems, just the family and nature getting along in harmony. Of course the two plus acres did need to be cleared. It was solid palmettos, some pine trees, and a generous population of cabbage palms.

There was certainly no hurry with the clearing. We were comfortable uptown and the kids didn't really want to move. Over a period of about one year, with an ax, a grub hoe, and a shovel, the lot was cleared. People probably though I was nuts, but this method provided exercise, protected the trees, and allowed me to keep an accurate scoreboard of poisonous snakes eliminated.

Had the clearing been done the customary way with a bulldozer, few of the snakes would have been seen and the potential population could not have been determined. Perhaps some were just passing through and were not permanent residents, but the figures show what might be found on two plus acres.

With the lot cleared and grass growing the final scoreboard tally read:

26 Pygmy Rattlers
4 Diamondbacks
4 Coral Snakes

I must admit to a couple of close encounters that caused me to put the tools away and quit working early in the day. When you step within three inches of a pygmy rattler and he doesn't strike, you have just about used up your luck for that particular day. One diamondback skin hangs over the fireplace and I still have the rattles from another that the horse killed. At any rate, snakes are disappearing at a rapid rate. They don't make out very well on concrete and manicured lawns.

No telling what some folks will go through to avoid a little embarrassment. Dave and I were fishing, each in our own boat, down south around Hellen Blazes. I was ready to quit but Dave wanted to fish fifteen more minutes so I went on to the camp expecting him to follow shortly. Those fifteen minutes passed, then one hour and fifteen minutes, and when it became two hours and fifteen minutes I decided to go check on him. Dave was in sight when I got to my boat, so I simply waited for him on the fill. He didn't want to discuss his tardiness and was rather insistent that we immediately go inside and play a game of pool. It must have been two months later when Dave casually asked, "Did I tell you about the snake crawling up the foot of my motor and getting in the boat?" He had not told me of the incident and, in spite of my questions, refused to elaborate further.

Apparently, for he would never verify it, that day he was late was the day of the snake encounter. He must have bailed out of the boat and then found some way to get rid of the snake. With his clothes all wet he had to wring them out and hang them on the bushes to dry so he wouldn't have to answer embarrassing questions at the camp.

Then there was this time a middle-aged fellow and two boys rented a boat. Along about dusk they came in and, let me tell you, they were certainly in a hurry. All three of them dashed around unloading the boat and putting their gear in the car. It just didn't look right, so I walked outside and asked, "How are you doing?" The man replied that someone had been shooting at them and he wanted to get away from the place as quickly as possible. I offered to call the Sheriff's Department and even insisted on it, but he didn't want that. I helped them load the rest of their gear and they were gone.

Back inside the camp, I got to thinking that something still just wasn't right so I went out to look at the boat. Two holes were visible in the bottom and one hole off to the side. All three were below the water line. Nobody can shoot at you and put holes in the bottom of your boat. Apparently a snake fell in the boat, the old boy became excited, started shooting, and didn't quit until he had put three holes in the bottom. No wonder he was in a hurry to leave and didn't want me to contact the Sheriff's Department. Henry might ask him to pay for the damage.

Snake events are unending, but most of them would have been of little importance if the involved people had not become excited. I had been fishing down south and was returning to the camp when I encountered two good old boys who fished that area often. I stopped for a moment to visit and found that due to yard work and such, they were very late getting out and had just started fishing. Nearing the camp I was very much surprised to see them coming in behind me, running at full speed. Without a word of explanation they loaded the boat as fast as possible and headed toward town.

It was about two weeks later when I ran into one of them and he asked if anyone had told me what happened that day. I hadn't been told anything, so he went on to explain. Seems a snake somehow managed to get in their boat. Now these guys always carried a twenty-two revolver with them, but this day they should have left it at home. The other fellow became excited, grabbed the twenty-two, and started shooting. The first shot didn't do much damage, just put a hole in the bottom of their new bass boat. The second shot did a little better—it not only put another hole in the boat, it also took off one of the shooter's toes.

They became a little more sensible at this point, beat the poor snake to death with a paddle, and headed for the hospital emergency room. It was probably a harmless water snake anyway.

Several years ago I took my old buddy Hutch fishing. Hutch didn't ask for much, just a pleasant day's fishing on the river with no expectation of catching the largest bass in the St. Johns or filling a cooler with fish. His only request was that I not position him in a bunch of snakes. He wasn't afraid of snakes but simply didn't like them. Midway through the day I ran Hutch's end of the boat up in the muck to keep it from moving and resumed fishing. Hutch sat there for quite some time then finally said calmly, "What did I tell you?" There, about one foot from him was a huge snake, which appeared to be a cottonmouth. Hutch didn't get excited, I backed the boat off the muck, and we found another place to fish.

Billy, Jeff, and I were fishing Hellen Blazes and, at the time, I carried a pistol in the tackle box. It was foolish to carry the gun—I couldn't hit anything with it, but others had somehow convinced me that it was needed for protection against all those wild creatures on the river. We encountered a huge cottonmouth and the boys insisted that I shoot it. The end result was that I emptied a clip of ammunition and the snake didn't even know it had been shot at.

Mafia Fishing Trip

LET ME SAY THAT THERE IS ABSOLUTELY no proof that the term "mafia" should be applied to this fishing trip. These folks may have operated nursing homes, as they professed, or they may have been visiting Sunday school teachers from Chicago. I simply don't know. However, after spending twelve unpleasant hours with them, it became obvious that they were not just common, everyday people.

On those rare occasions when the camp had need for a fishing guide, I was usually called upon. And, as a general rule, guide trips were pleasant, uneventful affairs, often with extremely interesting and enjoyable people. It's no secret, the more congenial the fisherman, the harder a guide works to put them on fish. That might help explain why this particular trip produced exactly zero fish, while the next resulted in a young man returning to Tennessee with a trophy bass—what we call a "wall hanger."

The phone rang rather late this evening and it was Henry wanting to know if I could guide a party the next morning—very short notice and Henry didn't provide any details. What the heck, no matter, it was about time for a day off from work anyway. Looking back, I still wonder. Was Henry aware of what he was getting me into?

Arriving at the camp next morning, I still didn't learn much about my fishing party. There were four fishermen and they wanted to fish Lake Hellen Blazes. Henry was to provide four dozen shiners, two cases of iced down beer, at least eighteen pork chop sandwiches, and one boat. I was to furnish the second boat. Offhand, it sounded like a fun group.

It wasn't yet daylight when a car pulled in the camp, and what a car it was, a long, shiny black stretch Cadillac. My fishermen had arrived so, unsuspecting, I went outside to meet them. First, there was a heavy-set, loud-mouthed man who obviously was the head honcho since he immediately started barking orders. Next there were two small, nervous, skinny guys wearing glasses. They jumped and trembled when the big man shouted. And finally, a chauffeur, complete with cap and jacket. The chauffeur was a big, mean-looking dude.

The trunk of the limousine held all sorts of expensive fishing tackle, but that wasn't as amazing as the huge back seat. It contained, among other things, a large, well-stocked, built-in bar and a TV. This mind you, was years ago, when a TV in an automobile was almost unheard of.

When I introduced myself, the boss man didn't hesitate to shout meaningless orders at me. My first reaction was to tell him, "Kiss my Evinrude!" but remembering Henry's investment in shiners, beer, and sandwiches, this thought was dismissed. What a start. It was pure bedlam with the big man shouting unnecessary instructions and people stumbling over one another trying to accomplish the simple task of loading the boats. In all this hurry and confusion I failed to think of food and beverages for myself. That should have been no problem—they had loads of sandwiches and beer. Boy, did this prove to be a very poor assumption on my part.

The chauffeur replaced his uniform cap and jacket with a fishing cap and regular jacket. Funny thing, both jackets bulged in the same area, about where a person might carry a gun. He had never operated an outboard, so with some brief instructions and a short trial run, we were ready to go.

The boss man, noticing my fishing rod in the back of the boat asked, "What the hell is that for? I'm paying you to guide, not fish!" Rather than say what I thought, I replied, "Can't ever tell, we might need it."

It was wintertime, with occasional cold fronts and the weather so screwed up that there was no consistently good fishing. I like for the fishermen to know beforehand what to expect, so I tried to explain this to the boss man as we headed out. He quickly informed me that he had his shiners, he had fished Lake Hellen Blazes years ago with his daddy, and all I had to do was get him to the lake. He would take care of catching the fish.

After a thirty-minute boat ride to the lake, I simply went where he pointed, moved when he said, and stopped where he indicated. Not much going on for a few hours except for the pork chop sandwiches and beer—both were disappearing at an unbelievable rate. Talking seemed to be forbidden until the wimpy guy in our boat mumbled something about how poor the fishing was. This was a mistake. The fat boy lashed out with some choice comments including, "Oh shut up, you said the same damned thing when we were in Spain!" Even though we weren't on speaking terms, curiosity compelled me to ask, "You guys fished in Spain?" Given an opportunity to brag, the boss man replied, "We have fished all over the world—Spain, Mexico, Alaska, South America, you name it."

It was downright boring. All rigged the same and fished in the same manner. Obviously, when the big man offered a suggestion, it was not that at all, it was an order. With a bit of helpful advice, they could have caught fish, but the man didn't want a fishing guide, only a boat operator. Actually, it was somewhat comical, if you can picture four grown men fishing the poorest territories available. Almost as though they didn't want to catch fish. What wasn't the least bit humorous was that vanishing stack of sandwiches and cold beer. I hadn't been offered a sample of either.

Midway through the afternoon the boss man broke the silence with, "If you are such a good fisherman, let's see you catch something." I had expected something like this to happen and I was loaded with confidence, but the results of that first cast surprised even me. The instant my small homemade lure touched the water, it was inhaled. After a brief scrap, a small one-and-a-half-pound bass was alongside the boat. Not bragging size by any means, but it did make an impression. When I released the fish, the boss man, temporarily losing his temper, shouted, "Put that damned rod away!"

Back to the same routine, moving from place to place, fishing those shiners. Now I have nothing against shiner fishing. Like other methods, however, it should be done properly. These clowns, it would be safe to say, knew absolutely nothing about shiner fishing.

There wasn't a great deal of time left when the boss issued another challenge, "Bet you can't do that again." I didn't do as well this time. It took three casts before I landed another bass the same size as the first. Once again, I was told, in no uncertain terms, to put my rod away.

Perhaps this late in the day, I had become softhearted. Whatever—I offered to provide each of them with one of my small lures. They might yet be able to salvage a respectable catch of bass. The man, as if to prove he was still the boss, snarled something about what I could do with the lures then added, "We came out here to fish shiners and that is what we are going to do!" My gesture must have had some effect though, since he offered me one of the few remaining pork chop sandwiches and a beer. I might add, if pork chop sandwiches don't seem impressive at five in the morning, try one late in the afternoon, after a full day on the water with nothing to eat.

They now seemed resigned to not catching any fish and it was simply a matter of using up the remaining daylight. The boss man certainly hadn't become sociable, but he at least would talk a little. I asked what type of business he was in, not expecting an honest reply. He said, very briefly, "I operate nursing homes." Now, if operating nursing homes required a gruff, mean, obnoxious boss man, a couple of accountants, and a bodyguard, there was no reason to doubt his statement.

Back at the camp, unloading the boats and stowing the gear was accomplished without a hitch since the boss man immediately crawled into the huge back seat of his limousine, flipped on the TV, and started making himself a drink. The chauffeur changed back to his uniform, and the shiny black Cadillac eased out the driveway without so much as a "So long, kiss my foot," or anything else.

This was not my most enjoyable guide trip by any means. It remains however, the most unusual and memorable.

He Caught the Little One

ACTUALLY HIS NAME, ROBERT, DIDN'T FIT HIS LIFESTYLE. With a houseboat on the St. Johns River as home, he was a regular Huckleberry Finn, so let's call him Huck.

Huck and his father lived on the boat tied up across the road from the fish camp. Not one of those modern-day ritzy boats with all the accessories, theirs was a homemade affair floating on fifty-five-gallon steel drums. Grownups may have found the accommodations lacking, but what more could a youngster ask for. Huck could fish from the porch and had a boat available when he wanted to use it.

When school was in session, Huck's daily routine was ideal, always plenty of companionship. His buddies coming out from town on weekends and sometimes after school while others visited to fish off the porch.

Now school was out and Huck was having trouble keeping himself entertained. His father was at work, there were no other youngsters around, and he couldn't go anyplace since it was several miles to town. So other than fishing, there was little to occupy his time. Huck was not a loner by nature and regardless of how much a person likes to fish, having nothing else to do, day in and day out, will soon take the enjoyment out of your favorite sport. He continued to fish, but not often and with little enthusiasm. Fishing had now become simply a convenient way of passing time.

Huck, carrying his fishing rod, came into the camp to ask, "Mister Henry, how much is a shiner?" Henry teasingly explained that shiners came by the dozen, not by the each. The kid said all he had was a dime and could he get one shiner with that? Henry picked out one nice big shiner, which Huck placed in a paper cup filled with water and with no further conversation departed in the direction of the old bridge.

We should have been more curious, but Huck and his one shiner didn't arouse much interest among those in the camp. Imagine everyone's surprise when, only five minutes later, Huck was back carrying a huge bass!

We were far more excited than Huck, who seemed to be taking it as an everyday occurrence. Henry carefully placed the fish on the scale, which registered a whopping eight and a half pounds. With everyone complimenting him on this spectacular catch, Huck's only comment was a disappointed, "I wish I could have caught the big one."

Now wouldn't that remark arouse your curiosity?

The story had to be pried from him for Huck was no braggart and all this sudden attention had become embarrassing.

With considerable persuasion, Huck reluctantly explained that he had been out walking on the old bridge, simply killing time, when he noticed two bass lying near a small patch of weeds. In Huck's words, a big one and a little one. That is when he came to the camp for his one shiner. Returning to the bridge, he rigged the shiner and carefully dropped it in front of the big bass. To Huck's complete surprise and disappointment, the little bass dashed from the weeds and inhaled his bait!

Huck, no doubt, is the only Florida fisherman ever to land a little bass that weighed eight and a half pounds. Speculation on the size of the larger fish could go on and on, but one thing is certain, Huck would not lie or exaggerate. If he said it was big as compared to the fish he landed, it was *big*.

Now as far as Huck was concerned, his fishing was finished. The fish he landed hadn't excited him and prospects of catching one much larger no longer held any interest. Too much of a good thing—that boy was bored with fishing.

Those in the camp would not hear of this however. Take that fish to the houseboat and put it on ice to show your dad, then get back out there and catch the big one. This time Huck was supplied with three fresh shiners in a bait bucket, courtesy of his fish camp fans. The second try for Mr. Big proved to be very disappointing, certainly more so for those in the camp than for Huck himself. Being unable to again locate the monster, he fished only a short while, then became disgusted and quit.

That would have been the end of this event, except—

Later in the day, with more people present and Huck's catch temporarily forgotten, two fellows came in from fishing. Obviously overly equipped, they had a large expensive boat, a huge outboard motor, racks of fishing rods, three tackle boxes each, a depth finder, and an electric trolling motor. These two were not at all bashful about showing off their catch which consisted of three yearling bass, hardly worth keeping, a three pounder, and their prize, their braggin' fish, a six pounder.

What is it about excessively equipped fishermen that makes them feel superior? Perhaps they actually believe those advertisements that caused them to purchase such an accumulation of unnecessary tackle. Anyway, these extremely knowledgeable fishermen were willing to share their expertise. Another of those free fishing clinics.

One thing for sure, none of those present wanted fishing lessons of any sort. Old Herb apparently could take only thirty minutes of fishing school since he slipped out unnoticed, then reappeared escorting Huck, who just happened to be carrying his bass. Herb's only remark to the strangers was, "You guys must be doing something wrong. This young fellow, not even old enough to require a license, was only out five minutes with a cheap fishing rod and one shiner."

End of fishing clinic! Huck returned, once again, to the houseboat, this time with a free soda and candy bar.

Tex's First Ride

IT MATTERS LITTLE TO MOST FOLKS that the old timey fish camp atmosphere is a thing of the past. Gone—like the Dodo bird and the dinosaurs. A casual observer of modern-day Florida fish camps might assume there have always been throngs of tourists, fishing tournaments, sightseeing boat rides, and the like. Nothing could be farther from the truth. Facts are, some years back, none of these features were even slightly evident at any of the local camps. There were occasional tourists, of course, but, for the most part, fish camps survived through the patronage of local folks. Survived, incidentally, is a fitting term—none could be called prosperous. Weekends and holidays produced the most activity since virtually everyone worked, and with all this activity came perhaps a little bit of carelessness. No single weekend went by without the occurrence of at least one unusual, sometimes ridiculous event. It was easy to understand why this easygoing group had gotten to accept almost everything as routine. An airboat stuck in the marsh, one sunk in rather deep water, a broken prop or blown jug miles from the camp—none of these were worthy of a great deal of excitement. Those in a position to help simply did so, and normally the problem was soon corrected.

This relaxed attitude probably amazed outsiders, but after all, there were few of them. Although downplayed at the time, all these events, like Tex's first ride, were never completely forgotten.

A dozen or so of us were at the camp this particular Saturday afternoon, all pretty well worn out from fishing, boat riding, and such when a large rental car pulled in and parked. Little attention was paid until this dude came through the back door. He was a sight—a regular fashion plate! There could be no doubt that this guy had more invested in his wardrobe than some of the fellows had in their airboats.

A jacket that must have cost two hundred dollars, boots made from snakeskin or some other exotic material, light cream-colored, tailor-made trousers, a shirt that was the fanciest ever seen hereabouts, and a bolo tie, complete with a silver Texas Longhorn clasp. He looked like a walking advertisement for some high-class men's clothing store. By contrast, the regulars seldom shaved on weekends, wouldn't consider wearing anything other than work clothes, and were, by then, showing additional signs of wear and tear from the day's outing.

Certainly no one expected this classy stranger to remain in our midst for long. Especially since after buying a beer he produced a handkerchief to carefully brush off his chair before sitting down. While those in the back were still snickering, to the amazement of everyone he immediately joined in the general conversation with such friendliness that, other than outward appearance, he could have been mistake for one of the group. Not the slightest bit obnoxious or pushy, simply curious. He was from Texas, obviously, and since this was his first visit to the Sunshine State, he had many questions. Tex was, in spite of his fancy clothes, an all-around good fellow and everyone took an immediate liking to him.

He had never seen a gator in the wild, knew nothing whatsoever about local fishing, had heard somewhere of the St. Johns River, but other than the name, knew absolutely nothing about it. Tex was especially fascinated by all the airboats presently sitting quietly on the riverbank. How fast will they go? What type engines do they have and what are their horsepower? Will they, unlike regular boats, actually operate in the marsh? How much would a good one cost? With Tex showing such an interest in airboats, it was only a matter of time until one of the fellows offered him a ride. Now, Tex hadn't expected this turn of events, so he was kind of caught between a rock and a hard place. Briefly at a loss for words, he eventually mumbled, "No, I better not. We can put that off for some other day." This, of course, did not set too well with his newfound buddies, who insisted that an airboat ride on the St. Johns River would be the highlight of his Florida visit. Something to be remembered and talked about for years. With the encouragement of twelve river rats, Tex didn't stand much of a chance. It would only be a short, twenty-minute ride to Lake Sawgrass, and after all, he might just like airboating well enough to find use for a boat of his own back in Texas.

Most everyone went outside to see Tex take off, on what should prove to be a new, thrilling experience. He seemed a bit edgy, but that was to be expected. That fancy jacket and all certainly added a touch of class to the sport of airboating.

We, to a man, subscribe to Murphy's Law. If something can go wrong, it will go wrong.

It wasn't a huge surprise, but did seem a bit strange when only a few minutes after departing the boat could be seen returning to the camp. This was cause for many comments, but what the heck, a short ride is a short ride. When the two climbed out of the boat, however, it was apparent that all had not gone as planned. More soaked, muddy, mucky individuals have probably never been seen entering the camp!

Time out here to explain—no one has ever been totally wet, dirty, and completely messed up until he or she has gone overboard in the St. Johns River marsh. The only reasonable comparison might be those girls sometimes seen mud wrestling on TV, but such a comparison would be completely unfair—the girls use clean mud.

The ride to Sawgrass had been enjoyable. Tex was able to spot many of the critters—birds, fish, turtles, gators, and snakes—that he had been promised. Now getting a feel for airboating, he relaxed his firm grip on the seat and began to enjoy his surroundings. Riding the marsh alongside of Sawgrass was an experience Tex would never forget. So many things to see as they flushed flocks of birds and caught a glimpse of an otter. With all these things to see, there was something they didn't see—a hidden mud tussock. The boat stopped cold but the passengers didn't. Both went sailing out to land head first in two feet of St. Johns River muck! The boat obediently sat there idling, waiting for someone to shove it off the tussock, which the two did before crawling back in to conclude Tex's first airboat adventure.

There was absolutely no damage done. Well—one might consider Tex's clothes, but still, it was just a routine event around the fish camp.

Back at the camp, Tex accepted the dunking very good naturedly, even joining in with the joking about the current condition of his formerly spotless, fancy wardrobe. His partner had waded down the boat ramp to wash the worst of the muck off, but since Tex showed no intentions of doing the same, someone showed him to a hose. Maybe it was the odor of the sulfur water, but he didn't manage much of a clean-up job with the hose either.

Tex remained with us a short while longer, but would not sit down and, apparently didn't feel comfortable standing there dripping muddy water on the floor. Although everyone assured him he would soon dry out and there was no question that Tex would have liked to stay, he simply could not tolerate being in such a condition.

Looking back, Tex almost certainly would have become a valued member of our small select group has his indoctrination not been so hurried and abrupt.

After placing some newspapers on his car seat, Tex left us with one parting statement: "Fellows, I want you to know, I have not been on one airboat ride, I have had two—my first and my last!"

The Search

SOME EVENTS THAT WE NOW LAUGH ABOUT weren't the least bit funny when they occurred.

It was rather late one Sunday evening, maybe nine thirty or so, when two cars, absolutely crammed with women and children, pulled into the fish camp. A few of us old regulars were just visiting and Henry was about to shut down for the night when this gang burst through the back door. Everything from babies to grandmas with all the kids crying and some of the women nearly hysterical. They were all so upset it was some time before one of them settled down enough to explain their dilemma. Three men, sons, husbands, and fathers of the group, had gone out on an airboat at daylight and should have returned long before dark. The women had, without success, called everyone who might know of their whereabouts and now, upon arriving at the camp, they had found the men's truck and trailer parked on the fill. Something terrible must have happened!

We certainly couldn't provide any information. Those of us who had been on the water had not seen an airboat with three men, and a vehicle parked overnight was not at all unusual. Froggers stayed out all night and many airboaters went to camps up and down the river. We could only suggest they report the situation to the Sheriff's Department.

Our suggestion resulted in a big huddle around the telephone with everyone talking at the same time, total confusion. After quite some time the phone conversation ended and one of the ladies announced the Sheriff's Department would indeed conduct a search, but it very likely would not start until daylight.

This of course brought on more wailing and moaning and a strong suggestion, almost a demand, that some of us present start an immediate search. Unfortunately, at the time mine was the only boat available that was in running condition. Logically the airboaters had probably broken down, and with a little information I should be able to find them and tow the boat in. So much for logic—volunteering without asking where the men might be located was a huge mistake.

Not one of the entire group had any idea where the men had intended to go. Those fellows might be anywhere between Fellsmere Grade and Lake Poinsett, fifty or sixty miles of river and lakes. A question and answer session produced no information until someone mentioned Lake Hellen Blazes. Then one, and eventually all, agreed that they had heard the men discussing that particular lake. Now that wasn't much to go on, but it was a start.

Running in the darkness was no particular problem for anyone who spent a great deal of time on the river. Bushes, trees, stumps, and weeds, anything recognizable along the shoreline, informed you constantly of your location. Of course, there were some among us who never developed any powers of observation, but such folks may have gotten lost searching for the restroom at a local service station.

With an operation of this nature, you were not looking for a boat in the darkness, you tried to locate the missing men by sound. Run a mile or so, then shut the motor off and listen. Let out a few hollers, listen for a reply, then move on another mile or two and repeat the process. Let me tell you, it took a lot of hollering between the camp and the south end of Lake Hellen.

About two hours and thirty miles later I returned to the camp, having seen or heard nothing of the missing boaters.

During my absence, the family members had called several people and were now convinced the men had gone north, maybe Lake Washington. You see, some of us are slow learners. So once again, I allowed myself to be talked into resuming the search.

Bob wanted to go along on this trip, so the two of us set off for Lake Washington and points north. About the time we reached the center of the lake, fog started setting in, and by the time we reached the north end I could hardly distinguish Bob in the front of the boat. I shut the motor off, fired up a cigarette, opened a beer, and checked my watch. It was two thirty in the morning, we hadn't seen or heard anything, the fog was as thick as pea soup, and the search at this point seemed plenty ridiculous.

Bob was all for going on. In fact, if it was alright with me, he would run the boat and, if necessary, go all the way to Route 520, some thirty miles further north. Now, Bob had a reputation. A good friend and darned nice guy, he could get lost on a narrow stretch of the river in broad daylight. Bob owned an airboat for a while but never took it out alone since, most likely, he would not be able to find his way back. We switched places, Bob started the motor, then left it in neutral as he glanced around in all directions. There was nothing to be seen but fog. After a bit he said, "Maybe you better give me hand signals from up front and I'll go where you point."

We crossed the lake and hit the river mouth dead center, then had to maneuver through the fog where faint lights could be seen. Bob quieted the motor long enough to remark, "Man, we must have been moving to get to 520 this quick!" With the nose of the boat on the bank and us ready to get out, Bob finally realized what had happened, "We are not at 520, we are back at the fish camp!"

While we were gone an interesting thing happened. You couldn't call it foolish because it was downright dumb when Woody and Jeff cranked up Henry's old eighteen horse motor to join in the search. The motor would run perfectly for maybe two or three hundred yards, then it would quit and could not be restarted until it had completely cooled down, an hour or so later. So sure enough, about two hundred yards beyond the bridge the outboard stopped running and they had to return against the current with paddles. Now came the good part! Believe it or not, they were greeted by the mothers, wives, and children of the three lost men and presented with a twenty dollar bill for their efforts.

Enough of this searching for three people when we had no idea where they were, the fog so thick you couldn't cut it with a knife, and by now it was approaching 4:00 A.M.

I was out a night's sleep, a few gallons of gasoline, having traveled nearly fifty miles, and had to be at work by 7:00 A.M.

There was a happy ending however. About 8:30 the next morning the Sheriff's Department found the lost men on a houseboat in Lake Winder. Their airboat had quit running early in the day so they simply tied up to the houseboat, and with ample provisions, waited and slept, safe and comfortable.

Someone may find a needle in a haystack, and a blind hog will sometimes find an acorn, but don't search for overdue boaters in the dark when no one even knows which direction they went.

Bugs

ALL INSECTS ARE BUGS, but all bugs are not necessarily insects, if you recall Watergate.

We are blessed with an abundance of bugs—some good, some not so good, and some, like the imported fire ant, absolutely detestable. For the most part though, bugs can be tolerated. They come with the territory and certainly contribute their fair share toward fish camp stories. In addition, they may occasionally provide a little humor. Whether or not it is humorous, of course, depends upon whether you are an observer or the individual being stung or bitten.

Newcomers and tourists have trouble adapting to our plentiful supply of insects and they too may add a bit of humor to an otherwise routine afternoon at the camp.

A tourist was amazed to see two mud daubers flying around inside the camp and offered his opinion that all other activity should cease while everyone participated in annihilating those dangerous insects. He failed to see that the mud daubers were not harming anyone, and had he stepped out on the porch, there were thousands more, none of them creating problems. Now if you are at the Ritz in New York City, chances are there will not be any mud daubers flying around your table. If you are at the fish camp, it is a whole new ball game.

While on the subject of mud daubers, you may hear someone say that mud daubers do not sting. One way to put a stop to this foolishness is an offer to catch one for that optimist to handle. His or her education, regarding mud daubers, has been sorely neglected.

The lowly palmetto bug is often good for a laugh. It is amazing how many nice old ladies will confide in you that their houses are roach free, but they do have palmetto bugs.

This visiting dignitary had been assigned the choice apartment in the complex. Her luggage had just been delivered and the hostess was explaining all the grand features of the facility when a big old palmetto bug raced across the floor. The presentation was temporarily interrupted while the hostess thoroughly explained that it was not a roach, it was a palmetto bug. The dignitary, having lived in Florida some years back, simply smiled and said nothing. You can call them horseflies if you want, but a roach is a roach.

Something good can be said about most bugs, but not so with the fire ant. Can't remember one humorous incident involving fire ants unless you count that time a bunch of them tried to crawl inside the cast on the Old Man's broken ankle. Fire ants can be eliminated—a fact demonstrated four or five times a year on everyone's lawn. There are many products advertised as fire ant killers and they will all work to one degree or another. One fire ant killer was applied daily per the instructions and each following day would find the ant mound moved and reestablished ten feet or so from its previous location. This was a fire ant killer apparently formulated to make those little rascals walk themselves to death.

For whatever it's worth, we will pass along a fire ant eradication process guaranteed by one of the guys to be totally effective. Liberally apply several tablespoons of grits to each ant hill. That's it—sit back and await the results. As our amateur bugologist explains, ants will eat the grits, immediately become thirsty, and consume a great deal of water. The water, of course, causes the grits to expand and the little buggers simply blow up. This method, per our informant, has one minor drawback. He is a light sleeper and those miniature explosions throughout the night caused him to lose considerable sleep.

Anyone can stumble onto a fire ant hill with results that are, to say the very least, a thrilling experience. About the time a number of them have crawled up your leg, the leader gives a signal and they all bite at once. Fancy footwork, slapping, and brushing are in order, but regardless, they will still register a goodly number of bites.

Often when the marshes have recently flooded, airboaters forget about the fire ants. Those ants will, one way or another, survive. They crawl up on brush or anything available to get above the water and an unwary airboater may find himself and his boat full of hostile ants, which—once again, on signal—will start biting.

There is no shortage of chiggers, or red bugs, whichever name is preferred. Simply pull up under a willow tree on the edge of the lake during a shower. Next day it is evident that the little willow was home to at least ten thousand chiggers.

A favorite is the little fuzzy jumping spider. He is electrifying and the bite will definitely get your attention. The bite of this spider always feels as though you have touched a hot wire carrying 110 volts and that jolt has been known to make people come out of their clothing. It may be embarrassing, but there is no choice. He will keep biting until you get rid of him.

Have you ever heard someone make the statement, "Mosquitoes don't bite me?" Seems I have heard it from various sources for years, and it has been my policy to discount any such claims. Perhaps the person has never been exposed to a large, hungry swarm of the insects, and, of course, mosquitoes do not affect all people to the same extent. One person may scratch furiously and have welts remaining hours later, while another simply brushes them away and the irritation is gone in minutes. Taking all the various factors into consideration, I had no trouble with the statement, "Mosquitoes don't really bother me," but for a person to flat out say, "Mosquitoes don't bite me"—this was more than I could handle. Until!

It was late evening when I tied the boat up on the fill and began unloading my fishing gear as rapidly as possible. The mosquitoes were at their worst. You could brush one arm and kill a dozen of those pesky insects. In the midst of my hurried stowing of tackle, Miss Kentucky, wearing shorts, sauntered out of the camp to inquire about my fishing success. While I rushed back and forth to the truck, flailing away at the mosquitoes, she stood there talking about fishing and not swatting the first time. I said, "You better get back inside, these mosquitoes will eat you up." She replied, "Mosquitoes don't bite me." Examination revealed that, while I had no less than fifty mosquitoes on various parts of my anatomy, there was not even one on the young lady.

I can now honestly say that I have met at least one person that mosquitoes would not bite. Now let me tell you about the honey bee on the beer can caper. There is a serious side to this story and it is not restricted to honey bees since yellow jackets and wasps, at times, will behave in the same manner. You may or may not believe that a honey bee will become intoxicated, but let me assure you, under certain conditions they will.

A honey bee has no desire to harm anyone. It just goes about doing a job of making honey, pollinating plants, trees, and all that, but at times may become thirsty. This particular bee—let's name him Buzzy—was a good fellow, but the best laid plans of mice, men, and bees sometimes go astray.

With a group of us gathered at picnic tables in the park, one lonesome little honey bee decided to join the crowd. Buzzy may have been around the park for some time and perhaps was a good candidate for AA treatment, I have no way of knowing for certain. People were drinking various soft drinks, and there were no less than three different brands of beer available, but he chose to land on Junior's can. Probably his favorite brand. Now Junior had been through this before and had a ready solution. He poured Buzzy a little puddle of beer on the table top and the bee left him alone. Like some humans, though, after awhile Buzzy became overly friendly, obnoxious, fearless, and a total bore. When Junior left, the little fellow decided he and I were buddies, so he laid claim to the top of my beer can. It didn't matter, I was also leaving. I chucked the can in the receptacle and was nearly to the truck when I heard Ol' Bill let out a squall. Buzzy had nailed him on the lip. I still say it was because Bill was drinking that outlaw beer, but it didn't matter. Within four days, Bill's lip was back to normal.

The honey-bee-on-your-beer-can event happens quite often with the result that many people are stung on the lip each year. Some have been known to swallow a bee—and wouldn't that get your undivided attention.

Pool

THIS DISSERTATION RELATES TO THE GAME that requires a table, cue sticks, a covey of numbered balls, and one white ball. It has nothing to do with swimming pools, which are actually holes in the ground that should be filled in at the first opportunity.

Times have changed, people have changed, and fish camps either changed or disappeared. Things are not as they once were when the fish camp was a meeting place, like the old neighborhood tavern, and the pool table often a center of activity.

That, my friends, is progress! We are now entitled to pay exorbitant property taxes, which, unquestionably, provide us with all the good things in life. That old two lane road, where you encountered few other vehicles, is now six lanes of bustling traffic. Huge fish kills are accepted as a natural occurrence, the scrub jay, gopher turtle, and manatee are headed for extinction, and a carefully planned retirement income becomes less sufficient with each passing month. If things get any better, we may not be able to stand it!

Enough of that, back to the pool table.

One old camp had a leaky roof, which didn't bother us rugged outdoorsmen in the slightest. If it dripped where you were sitting, you simply moved to an area where it was not dripping. After several months, however, with no attempt to fix the roof, the dry spots became few and at times rather crowded.

The pool table made out very well for awhile. There were a few drops here and there, but they could be wiped up with little or no interference to the pool game. Progressively though, the leaks worsened, and at times the table became well soaked. Efforts were made to cover the table, but this proved rather futile since the cover also leaked. Holes were made in the ceiling to detour the water and props were added, but in the end, it seemed all that leaking rain water was destined to land on the pool table.

The regular gang simply adapted and just went on playing. It was a bit more difficult considering a wet table, wet cues, wet tips, and wet chalk, but these disadvantages applied to all participants, so it equaled out. It was rather funny though, since when someone broke the balls and the cue ball went racing down the table, it was often followed by a little rooster tail, not unlike a miniature hydroplane.

The roof had been repaired but the pool table remained the same. So the rails were dead, the cloth worn, and the cue sticks crooked. These shortcomings handicapped all players equally so no on had reason to complain.

To its credit, the table served more than one purpose. It had, on occasion, been used as a bed. Probably not as comfortable as an expensive mattress, but considerably better than sleeping on the ground. And all that was needed for conversion to an excellent buffet table was the addition of a sheet of plywood.

Evenings and weekends usually found the pool table very busy with numerous players awaiting their turn. These were times of serious, intense rivalry, each shooter obsessed with only one thing—winning! Such an attitude is understandable, but definitely not conducive to enjoyment of the game.

Since throngs of people, overwhelming noise, and humorless pool were not our idea of fun, most of us old timers, avoiding the busy periods, visited the camp early on weekdays. We encountered few people, could converse without shouting, and normally had the pool table to ourselves. Our group also played to win, but certainly with no degree of seriousness. To us, making a good shot was more gratifying than actually winning the game.

Alas, with all our precautions, there were occasions when the peace and quiet, even our private pool games, were invaded.

There were only six people in the camp this weekday afternoon and conversation had nearly exhausted every subject when Ralph and George decided to shoot a few games. There was the usual banter, "I'll rack, you break," "No, I'll rack, you break," and then an agreement to flip a coin.

The outcome of the game was not at all important. For two quarters they would while away some time and still stay tuned to the continuing discussions concerning politics, football, cooking, fishing, sex, or whatever. None of those present were authorities on any of the subjects, but this minor disadvantage did not hinder the debate.

Now into their third game, each having won one, a stranger entered the camp, bought a beer, then very intently studied the pool game. An age-old story. If this stranger decided he was better than those playing, he would challenge the table.

It just so happened that Ralph was carrying a sizable amount of cash, receipts from his business that would later be deposited at the bank. Meanwhile, why not put that bankroll to use?

When George won the third game, Ralph uttered a few obscenities, pulled out his huge roll, selected a $100 bill, and disgustedly threw it on the table. George, as though on cue, nonchalantly picked up the bill and crammed it into his pocket. The next game was won by Ralph with the procedure being reversed, George doing the mumbling and throwing the bill on the table. After picking up the $100 bill, Ralph casually asked the stranger,

"You want some of this action? He's already into me for five hundred and I need some relief." The stranger, noticeably shaken by Ralph's invitation, declined while offering numerous excuses, then hurriedly finished his beer before departing.

So, having thus prevented an almost certain uninvited interruption, the game resumed to its usual innocence.

When Atlanta Al changed from his right hand to his left for a difficult pool shot, an onlooker excitedly exclaimed, "Looka there, that man is AMBIPHIBIOUS!"

Tall Turkeys

WILD TURKEYS SIX FEET TALL? Now, we of the fish camp fraternity do not claim that turkeys of that size exist. Indeed not, but we earnestly insist that they are not unheard of. The reason for this being two hours of conversation, one pleasant afternoon, during which we heard of nothing but tall turkeys.

First, Alabam should be introduced since it was his personal turkey tale that started the whole affair. Alabam, for the most part, was just another good old boy who could get along with almost anyone. He did, however, have one special talent. He was an accomplished agitator. A harmless, fun-loving individual, he was totally incapable of tolerating a routine, quiet, uneventful afternoon gathering. If nothing in particular was going on, you could bet your last dollar that he would make something happen. He could sometimes create more controversy in fifteen minutes than the entire congregation could get sorted out and settled down in a week. When asked where he was from, Alabam always replied, "LA." This was certainly true—he was from Lower Alabama.

Well anyway, let's get back to those huge turkeys. Alabam and his buddy came busting into the camp this extremely quiet afternoon with the profound observation that there were some turkeys peacefully feeding alongside Wickham Road. Everyone could accept wild turkey sightings, that was not unusual, but when Alabam insisted these birds were six feet tall, it appeared there might be some skeptics in the group.

Alabam, now with everyone's attention, explained in great

detail everything he had observed about the birds. He also insisted that all hunters present immediately load up and go bag those turkeys. They were walking around in an open field and should be easy pickings. Besides, one of them by itself would provide Thanksgiving dinner for at least two hundred people.

All this discussion went on for quite some time and might have consumed the entire afternoon except that someone asked the precise location of the birds. When Alabam pinpointed the area, the myth of six-foot-tall turkeys would have come to an end had it not been for the thoughtfulness of one individual. With Alabam all cranked up and on a roll, why stop now? This fellow suggested that the authorities should be notified of Alabam's amazing discovery, perhaps the Sheriff's Department. Alabam immediately agreed. Why hadn't he thought of that? He searched through the phone book, found the proper number, and invested a quarter in the pay phone.

Certainly the Sheriff's folks wondered what kind of a nut was on the other end of the line, but then they didn't know Alabam. For that matter, when he started talking about Wild Turkey, they may have assumed it had something to do with the kind that comes from a bottle.

Regardless of all that, Alabam patiently repeated all he had told us. This, of course, took awhile and he added one more small detail to emphasize his reason for calling.

"These birds are so large, they might be potentially dangerous." There followed a long-winded question and answer session that continued until Alabam, once again, specified the exact location of the birds, then all we heard from him was, "Uh huh. Uh huh. Uh huh." After hanging up the phone, Alabam treated us to an unnecessary thirty-minute explanation. Those weren't really turkeys, they were emus, a huge bird similar to the ostrich. And that area off Wickham Road was actually part of a wildlife sanctuary.

The Little Red Airboat

EVERYTHING CONCERNING THE LITTLE RED AIRBOAT was absurd. You couldn't tell what was going on until it had gone on!

There wasn't a single boat on the lake nor a vehicle in the parking area when a nice, shiny new pickup truck, towing a little red airboat, backed up to the county launching ramp. We at the camp recognized a great many who launched, but not this rig. The boat, truck, and the two men weren't at all familiar.

Not particularly interested in people we didn't know, the strangers were forgotten until they cranked up the airboats engine. It didn't require a mechanic's opinion that that little 65 was very, very sick. Oh well, they probably brought it to the lake only to work on it. No one would attempt to run a boat with the engine in such a sorry condition.

Now came the first of several surprises. We could hear the boat, but couldn't see it until it appeared around a point of weeds, headed for the open lake. With both of them on board and the engine running at full throttle, the boat was only traveling at six or eight miles per hour, but the transom, it was only an inch or so above water!

Why, if they couldn't get the boat to run properly, were they headed for deeper water in the open lake? Maybe they knew what they were doing, but it didn't seem likely. Offhand, it looked like a disaster looking for some place to happen.

While the boat plodded along, apparently headed for the dam, everyone voiced the same opinion. There was no way the two could possibly make a roundtrip without sinking. Among other things, any sort of turn would put the transom under water.

The others lost interest, but I continued to watch, and sure enough, when they reached the center of the lake, the deepest water and farthest point from either shoreline, down she went!

Fortunate that I was watching? Not for me it wasn't. If I hadn't been there they would probably have swum to the shoreline, waded to their truck, and abandoned the boat. This was only the beginning.

With my boat sitting in the stall ready to go, Ernie and I jumped in and took off. We didn't know what to expect, but if they had life jackets and could swim, they should be in no great danger. As we approached, they were indeed doing quite well, kind of paddling around, but there was no sign of life jackets or anything else floating. They appeared reasonably calm, until both tried to crawl in the boat on the same side. This would have capsized my boat and there would have been four people floundering around in the center of the lake. I kicked the boat in reverse and Ernie picked up a paddle and prepared to bash them on the fingers. From a little distance I shut the motor off and caution them. If they wanted to be picked up, come over the transom one at a time. With the two safely in the boat, I chucked the anchor out so as not to lose the location of their sunken boat, then asked, "Can't you guys swim? You were about to sink us getting in the boat." They informed us that they were excellent swimmers, and were in fact professional saltwater divers, but they were deathly afraid of snakes and gators.

Handing them a boat cushion with a short length of rope, I explained that we would have to mark the boat before leaving, otherwise it might require hours of searching when they came back to retrieve it. It was amazing how genuinely afraid the two were to get back in the water. They would just as soon abandon the boat. What kind of airboaters had I encountered who were so scared of snakes and gators? After assuring them time and again that there were no snakes or gators near our location, one of them finally relented and went back overboard to tie the cushion to the prop guard. He didn't waste a second getting back in the boat.

Not one word was said during the return to camp.

Back on dry land, my part of the foolishness should have been finished. Right? Not so, however. The two wanted advice. What should they do now? Didn't these guys know anything? All airboaters have a bunch of buddies they run with, so in a situation like this, the normal procedure is to call some of the fellows and organize a boat-raising operation. When I mentioned this, the two said they were from down south and didn't know a single person in the immediate area.

Along about here, we got a feeling that these fellows didn't want anyone to know their names, or precisely where they were from.

Well, what are you going to do? Two good old boys from down south and they didn't have a single friend nearby. Although it seemed unlikely that my kicker boat would raise the airboat, if they wanted, we would give it a try. They were very much in favor of this, so with a tow rope we went back out. Ernie wisely disappeared. Finding the marker was no problem, but once again, both were extremely reluctant to get back in the water. Eventually, the original volunteer again went overboard to attach the tow rope, then hurried back into the boat.

The first effort at towing was a total flop. Now they told me the boat was lying on its side. A little heated discussion—they should know there was no way I could tow the boat unless it was upright. Both of them would have to get back in the water and muscle the boat into the proper position. It took considerable reassurance that there were no snakes or gators nearby, but the two big brutes went back in the water, immediately righted the airboat, and were back in my boat.

On the second try, as I eased the throttle forward, that little boat popped to the surface and trailed along behind like a puppy on a leash. Things were looking great as we headed toward the launching ramp at a respectable speed. We had covered considerable distance before the airboat started sluing off toward the weeds. No surprise, this always happens, so someone hangs on the transom to keep the boat level. Then you can continue in a straight line. I eased up on the throttle and let the boat settle to the bottom, now in shallow water with two or three feet of guard showing. When I explained that one of them would have to hang on the transom, this was met with a definite no way. Perhaps the center of the lake contained no snakes or gator, but the buggy whips were certainly full of them. They were deadly serious and there was no reason to discuss it further. I could have hung on the transom and let them run the boat, but from the mess they had made of things so far, that didn't seem sensible. I unhooked the tow rope and returned to the camp for a cold beer. The two strangers stayed off in a corner, quietly talking to each other.

Again, my part of this fiasco should have ended, but Paul and Fred, who had been observing this hour or so of frustrated effort, offered to help. They would tie their boat to mine and keep it on a straight course long enough to reach the launch ramp. It was a screwy-looking operation, but it worked as we made the remaining distance to the ramp.

The two could now hook the tow rope to the truck and pull the airboat the remaining fifty feet where it would be bailed out and loaded on the trailer. Everything worked fine as the boat eased up on the concrete ramp, but then the driver decided if he pulled it a little higher they could remove the plug to empty the water. This decision wasn't too smart. The fifty feet of nylon rope stretched, the eye in front of the boat gave way and went sailing like an unguided missile toward the rear window of the truck. Once again, luck was on their side. It sailed over the cab doing no harm whatsoever.

Mission accomplished, you might say, as I retrieved the rope and put the boat back in its stall.

It still wasn't finished. Once the boat was loaded, they needed more advice. Where could they have the boat worked on? They simply had to get it running again. More to get rid of them than for any other reason, I made a couple of phone calls and gave them directions to a shop where they might get some help.

During all this time, they had volunteered absolutely no information and now curiosity forced me to ask some obvious questions.

"How long have you been running airboats?"

"Today was the first time."

"How long have you had this boat?"

"We just got it. It was parked alongside the road with a for sale sign and we stopped and bought it."

"What did you pay for it?"

"A thousand dollars."

One more thing before they left. "There won't be anything in the newspaper about this will there?" They were assured that an airboat sinking wasn't really news hereabouts and that made them extremely happy.

If you summarize all this, it becomes very interesting and also very mysterious:

- They didn't want anyone to know who they were or where they were from.
- They attempted to run an airboat without any previous experience.
- They were totally unfamiliar with the territory other than, perhaps, the area they were trying to reach.
- They had no local airboat buddies.
- They knew virtually nothing about snakes and gators.
- They didn't want their sinking publicized.

At any rate, they went up the road to search for Jim, who might be able to get their boat running and our group settled back into its normal routine.

Now, with time to give it some thought, it appeared those two big old boys were in this part of the country to do a job. They apparently were supposed to pick up something in the marsh or river, and at this point had no way of reaching their destination.

The little red boat never returned, but late in the afternoon, a large, high-powered boat put in and went racing off toward the dam. They weren't back at dark, but their mission must have been a success since there was nothing in the newspaper.

So, you see, we sometimes had more excitement at the fish camp than flat tires, empty gas tanks, and stuck trucks.

Supermouse

THIS LITTLE EPISODE RELATES TO UNUSUAL PETS, which reminds me of several years back when I had a skunk. It would be nice to say a pet skunk, but he was not really a pet, he was mean. Bit me one time, with those extremely long, sharp teeth, on the index finger. All the way to the bone from both sides and it was quite some time healing. His name, appropriately enough, was Stinky, even though he was supposedly deodorized. Perhaps he couldn't store a supply of that potent perfume but he could still generate enough to get your attention.

Stinky was a neighborhood attraction. The kids would stop by on their way to and from school to visit with him. Had he adapted like a house cat, everything would have been fine. That was not to be and I have never since handicapped and penned any wild creature that would be better off left unmolested in its natural environment.

Heck, I would like to have a pet buzzard if he would just hang around and not create problems. I know the bird books say they are vultures, but for a goodly number of years they have been buzzards to me. They will therefore, in my vocabulary, continue to be buzzards.

While on the subject of buzzards, did you know that young buzzards in the nest are white, fluffy, cuddly little things? They sure are and that just shows to go you that growing up can be detrimental to anyone's or anything's appearance. Adult buzzards are definitely ugly!

All this, obviously, has nothing to do with Supermouse but

does relate to unusual pets and the caging of wild things.

An aquarium containing exotic fish appeared at the camp. Certainly nothing earth shattering about this. Doctors' and dentists' offices had fish in aquariums. Watching little fish in an aquarium is reported to be restful, soothing, and relaxing. Such therapeutic qualities appeared wasted however, since the fish camp gang only wanted to try the colorful little fishes as bass bait.

Some time later a second aquarium appeared but this one contained neither water nor fish—it was home to a large snake. There is some disagreement as to the species of the snake. Many are certain it was a boa constrictor, which would make the story more impressive, but I remember it as a common rat snake. Regardless of species, everyone agrees, the snake was at least four feet in length.

Now, if you are going to keep a snake penned in an aquarium you must feed him, and believe me, snake definitely do not eat table scraps. The local supermarket may have dog and cat food, but with snakes you stop by a pet store and purchase a couple of live mice.

So the lid was removed from the aquarium and two mice were unceremoniously dumped in. There wasn't time to name Supermouse's companion since the snake immediately nailed and devoured him. Our hero, visibly shaken, wisely retreated to the far corner of the aquarium.

Apparently that one meal was sufficient for the time being since the snake, showing no interest at all in Supermouse, curled up in a corner and obviously went to sleep.

That, my friends, was a fatal mistake!

After a period of time, Supermouse left his huddled up position and began to move about, investigating the entire interior of the aquarium. In his rambling he walked and crawled on the snake with absolutely no repercussions. The snake continued to sleep.

One certainly cannot say that a mouse is capable of thinking or reasoning, but the final outcome indicated that this mouse had made a decision not to become supper for the same snake that had consumed his companion.

Supermouse slowly and deliberately crawled up on the snake to reach a position behind its head, then suddenly sunk his teeth at the base of the snake's skull! There was no visible disturbance, no thrashing about as would be expected. The snake simply stiffened while the mouse hastily retreated to the far corner of the aquarium. It didn't seem at all logical that the small rodent's bite would prove to be fatal, but later examination revealed the snake was indeed quite dead.

For this display of bravery against innumerable odds, Supermouse earned his name and his freedom. Surely no one could wish further harm to the courageous little creature, so he was released at the edge of the marsh.

Unbelievable? Perhaps—but not to those who witnessed the encounter.

Boat Ramp Comedy

HUMOR, OFTENTIMES, DEPENDS UPON ONE'S PERSPECTIVE. An example would be the fellow who has been shopping in a crowded supermarket and after thirty minutes has finally made it through the check-out counter. He is now walking toward his car, both arms loaded with full shopping bags over which he can hardly see. In the equally crowded parking lot he encounters a friend who whispers, "Your fly is open."

That's the way it is on a boat launching ramp. Observers see things differently than those folks with the boats.

One of the guys has a recommendation that definitely deserves consideration. "For a morning or afternoon of entertainment at absolutely no expense, all that is needed is a lawn chair and a cooler filled with your favorite beverages. Select a nice shady spot near one of the popular launch ramps, sit back, and watch what happens."

Here come the boaters! The morning shift consists mostly of those putting in, and the afternoon shift, those taking out, but there is often a large mixture of both. Pity the poor guy who is trying to take his boat out while a large number are putting theirs in. He may have a court appointment, a plane to catch, or simply need to visit the restroom, but regardless of circumstances, his priority is the absolute lowest. The general attitude of those not yet on the water is that he has been out, has had his fun, is finished for the day, is in no hurry, and deserves no consideration.

Possibly most boaters are reasonably thoughtful and will await their turn to launch, but anyone showing the least bit of hesitancy will be immediately bypassed, and may find himself at the end of the procession. Lost tempers, foul language, and worse are common when a large number of boaters are backed up, waiting to launch.

Much could be said about the skills of those who launch boats, but basically all can be placed in one of three categories: those who know what they are doing, those who think they know what they are doing, and those who don't know what they are doing. On second thought, there may be only two categories. No matter really. All can provide amusement for serious ramp watchers.

Not the most prevalent, but certainly the most obvious, are those individuals who feel that all that is required to become a full-fledged, bona fide boater is simply buying a boat. This type normally knows nothing about the territory and little about his boat. He should know how to start the motor, how to steer, how to change speeds, and how to shut the motor off. Little more is expected. One unfailing trait of the beginner is to show up when the launch ramp is already overloaded with boats and frustrated people.

His turn comes with six others waiting behind him and friends—it is a sight to behold. Having no experience backing the trailer—that not considered a requirement for being a boater—he accepts this as an opportunity to hone his skills. Twisting and turning, back and forth, up and down the ramp, he manages, with ample, not too friendly advice from bystanders, to consume a considerable amount of time.

With the boat and trailer finally in the water, things are looking up when a slight problem arises! Our boater has forgotten to remove the tie-down strap. This will cause another minor delay while he pulls the boat back up the ramp—he definitely doesn't want to wade in and get his shoes wet. The trailer, still well lined up, is not too difficult to back into the water again. Now, however, another discovery! He has forgotten to install the drain plug and the boat is rapidly filling with water! Nothing to do but pull the boat out, once again, and allow it to drain on the slope of the ramp.

The waiting boaters are not totally silent throughout the strap and draining operations, but our beginner is apparently immune to verbal abuse, as the trailer is backed into the water for the third time.

Surely nothing more can go wrong. Right? Let's just watch and see.

Now he will load his equipment. Three coolers, fishing rods, tackle boxes, life jackets, and a portable radio. The latter is needed to disturb the peace and quiet out there on the lake. Oh yeah, don't forget the suntan oil and a couple of towels.

All this doesn't take long, but could have been accomplished while awaiting his turn on the ramp.

The boat is floated off the trailer without incident and our boater is now ready to park his vehicle. A piece of cake unless he has to back into a parking space. Meanwhile, his boat is still blocking the ramp, and you might say that the natives are becoming restless.

After parking he returns to the ramp only to find the boat keys are locked in the car. Another slight delay, which is insignificant really, since by now he has consumed forty-five minutes and the number of waiting boaters has increased from six to twelve. Eventually, he is off, amongst cheers reminiscent of a touchdown by the home team.

Gator Tales

THIS EVENT OCCURRED IN *1965*, several hundred miles from Brevard County, in a huge, wild, desolate, uninhabited area not particularly noted for its gator population. Everyone knew there were gators around, but they were seldom seen, and for the most part, simply ignored. Spring floods would often bring gators to the attention of the public when they were washed out of their normal haunts and newspaper accounts told of dangerous twelve and fourteen footers being destroyed because they had ventured into residential areas. Strangely enough, these were always large gators. Small gators were seldom seen, even by those who fished regularly.

This particular day, after a couple of hours of serious fishing, I decided to do some exploring. The very few who fished this desolate territory stayed in the open water and didn't bother with the various offshoot little branches. I might just find a previously undiscovered good fishing hole up one of those sloughs. Investigating a couple of them produced nothing significant. They were shallow, narrow, and not very long, dead-ending in areas of partially dry land with large trees. The third slough was little different, somewhat longer, maybe half a mile, and with a bit more depth, but upon reaching the inevitable dead end, I had found no sought-after secret fishing hole.

With barely enough room, I used the paddle to turn the boat around, then cranked the motor to idle through fallen tree branches, logs, and stumps. After some few hundred yards of this slow going, I noted a disturbance in the water ahead. No splashing, just ripples and small waves created by something large moving through the water. Drawing closer, the disturbance appeared to be caused by a gator. I eased on and shut the motor off for a better look. From twenty feet there was little to be seen. A gator for certain, but mostly under water. Then came a very surprising turn of events. Between the boat and the first gator, a second gator came to the surface—this was the big one! With his nose nearly touching one bank and his tail nearly touching the other, he effectively blocked the narrow ditch. It didn't seem wise to make any kind of disturbance with the huge gator only six feet away so I just sat and watched. The most impressive realization was the width of the gator—it looked to be four or more feet across its back. This, to me, was more startling than the creature's length. It still remains my most vivid memory of the entire experience—a back so broad that any gator I've seen since appears small by comparison.

A standoff for sure—the gator didn't move and I didn't move. After several minutes of this, the other gator, still nearly submerged and definitely smaller, made its way down the slough where its progress could be followed by a trail of bubbles. After perhaps fifteen minutes the big gator had not changed his position, so I made a few experimental dips with the paddle to see what his reaction would be. This didn't seem to faze him at all, so I lined the boat up parallel for a comparison of length. All this within six feet, mind you. With the boat lined up, that part of the gator showing above the water exceeded the fourteen-foot boat's length by two feet.

The stalemate continued, the big gator remaining in position to block my way back to open water, and I began to wonder how long this would go on. Easing the boat away with the paddle, I cranked the motor, thinking the disturbance might cause him to move. Idling in neutral had no effect whatsoever, but a few brief spurts in reverse, and then forward, caused small waves and old granddaddy gator sank from sight. In the shallow water, his trail could be followed by a line of bubbles that ended abruptly at the bank of the slough. He had obviously gone to his hidden gator hole up under the bank. Little wonder he was reluctant to move—I had invaded his private domain, and you might say, parked a boat in his front yard.

I kept my sighting secret for many years for fear that if word go out, someone would have killed the gator just so he could say he had killed one over sixteen feet. I have never divulged the location, though at one time, plans were underway for me to guide a group of alligator authorities to verify the existence of a sixteen-foot gator. This expedition failed to materialize, and though it is unlikely the big fellow is still alive, the location remains a secret.

Being that large, the gator was certain old at the time. I prefer to believe that he continued to avoid detection, living out his life unmolested.

With all my knocking around, on only two occasions have I seen gators act aggressively toward a boat. One, I felt, was a female guarding her nest. She did not move away from the boat, as is normal behavior, but instead moved toward the boat. I remained in the vicinity for a short while, moving the boat about, but regardless of which direction I went, she continued to follow. There was no point in disturbing her further so I left the area.

The other aggressive gator, encountered in the center of Lake Washington, had reason to be belligerent. This one appeared to be injured, with bloody wounds on top of its skull. As we approached with the boat, the gator actually charged. This was no problem since the boat could easily outrun the creature, but curiosity kept us around until it happened a second time, whereupon it was time to leave the vicinity.

If a similar event were to occur today, considering the number of people who use the lake, the authorities should be notified immediately. Back then, it was only an unusual item for fish camp conversation.

Of course, some people can be rather foolish around gators. Like the old boy who showed up each weekend with a bag of chicken necks to feed the small gators at the end of the boat stalls. He thought it was lots of fun until one of them got hold of his hand.

How, for gosh sakes, was the little gator to know where the chicken neck ended and the man's fingers began?

It's not every day that you see a tree-climbing gator. We were idling quietly around the edge of the lake conducting a personal survey of the gator population. If a person does this often enough, he can rather accurately predict the location and size of the larger ones. Also, if you are quiet and do not approach too closely, they aren't even disturbed. As we rounded a clump of buggy whips, I confidently predicted, "There should be a six footer sunning on the bank ahead." To my surprise, when we were in the proper position, no gator could be seen. He had been there regularly on previous trips. We slipped in for a closer look and Bob announced, "There he is," pointing to a slanted willow tree. Sure enough, there, a few feet above the water, was our six-foot gator. We had approached too closely though, so the gator released its hold and dropped into the water, making quite a splash.

When we told our story to the fish camp group, they threatened to call the men with the white coats and the large dip net.

Bird Tales

HOW MANY FOLKS HAVE SEEN a crow catch a full-grown dove and fly off with the dove clutched in its beak?

It was early spring, and two doves were going through a courtship routine while two crows sat on the fence nearby. Without warning, one of the crows swooped down, snatched up a dove, and went flying off into the trees with the dove wildly flapping its wings. The dove obviously escaped because immediately after going out of sight in the trees, the crow returned and resumed its position on the fence.

A surprising incident for me, and sure enough, a thrilling experience for the dove.

Saw an albino robin one time—not totally white, it had a few dark feathers. This was in early spring when large flocks gather, preparing to move north. With hundreds of birds in the yard, searching for insects and seeds, one was different from the others—an unfamiliar species. Sneaking around for a better view, I succeeded in getting pretty close, but still could not identify the bird. Then it emitted a brief chirp. Shaped like a robin, traveling in a huge flock of robins, and chirping like a robin, it must be a robin. I saw the bird for two consecutive days, then it apparently moved on.

Rather excited about this sighting, when I told others they

Flooded Lake Washington Resort.

Lake Washington Resort, 1967.

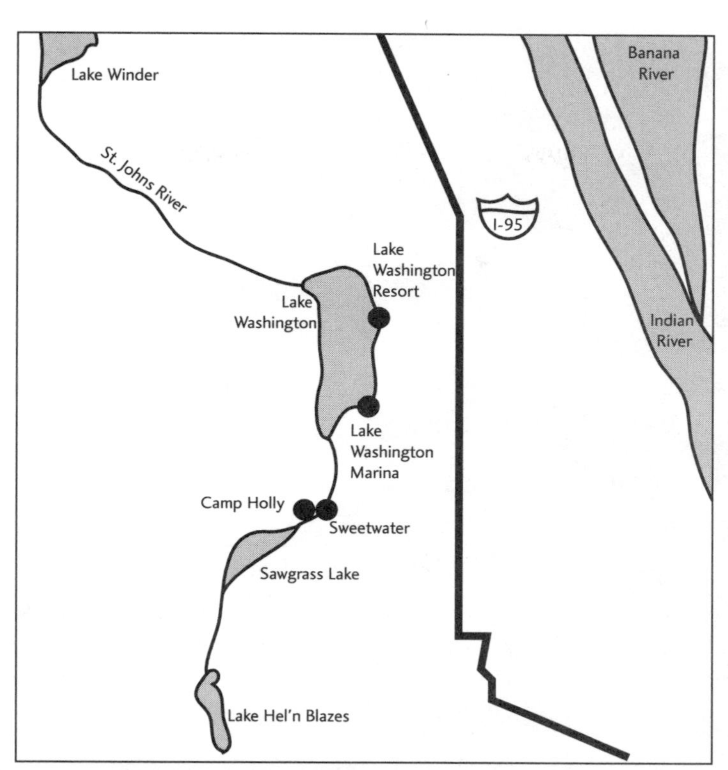

Quiet times at the resort.

Well armed. Let's hope a snake does not crawl into the boat.

Lone airboater awaiting his buddies.

The fish-cleaning table. Humans ate the fillets,
critters got the residue.

Lake Washington Conservation Association assistance boat.
A welcome sight to boaters in trouble.

Swapping stories.

Boat-a-cade to Fellsmere Grade.

The makeshift illegal Lake Washington dam in 1970.

Buckyboar.

informed me that albino robins were not all that uncommon. Well, being pretty observant and not exactly a spring chicken, I have seen a grand total of one albino robin.

Eagles in the front yard? Extremely exciting at first, but now, after several years, they are routinely expected during every nesting season.

We are fortunate to have an eagle's nest nearby and a pair of eagles that have adapted well to human encroachment. When mating season rolls around they return from somewhere and are often seen flying high in the sky. Very interesting, since their appearance is so predictable. Except during bad weather, they will be seen every morning, allowing us to surprise visitors by pointing out, "Those are our neighborhood eagles flying up there."

When they have young to feed, the adult eagles are kept extremely busy. It must be a daylight till dark effort to keep the little ones satisfied. Fish, of course, are their main source of food, and since the eagle is not well equipped to catch live fish, it depends heavily upon dead fish found along shorelines and the edges of ponds. It is during the birds' continuous feeding hunts that they may be seen near the front yard pond.

Our neighborhood is dotted with ponds in all directions—some large, some small, all very well stocked with fish. Due to various causes, mostly old age, fish will occasionally die and float to the surface. With such a large number of ponds the eagles have come to depend upon them for a handy food supply.

Joe, his pond absolutely loaded with a variety of all our common freshwater fish, decided to try raising goldfish. In order for such a project to be successful, he must first remove all the native fish. He trapped, netted, and moved a large number of fish, but even with the water level drawn down, could not completely clean the fish out and finally had to resort to poison.

Leaving for work the next morning, Joe checked the pond and found, to his amazement, the surface covered with dead fish. He would certainly be facing an undesirable task when he returned from work—there seemed to be bushels of dead fish to be gathered and buried. When Joe pulled into the driveway that afternoon, he received a pleasant surprise! In the trees nearby were ten well-fed wood storks and two adult eagles. Only four tiny fish remained floating on the pond.

During one nesting season, with tasty freshwater catfish readily available from Lake Washington, I would bring a number of the fish home, fillet them, and toss the carcasses in the pond. It never took long for our neighborhood eagles to spot them, and one by one, the carcasses were carried off to their nest.

From all this determined effort on the part of the parents, we have come to expect only one young eagle. Rarely there have been two. These juveniles are large, duplicates of the parents but lacking the distinctive white head and tail. They will first be seen flying rather high with one of the older birds. Flying lessons? Later they may be seen perched in trees around the pond, learning to feed for themselves perhaps.

One week, that is as long as we can expect to see the youngsters, then the entire family seemingly disappears, gone to wherever they spend the summer.

We occasionally see adult and juvenile eagles during the summer months, but the habits of these birds are so drastically different that they are not accepted as part of our neighborhood family. Ours, hopefully, will return again in the fall for yet another successful nesting season.

Screwy Winds

AREA RESIDENTS WOULD BE ABSOLUTELY AMAZED at the number of funnel clouds spawned over the St. Johns River Valley during any summer thunderstorm season. This is nothing to become concerned over, however, because rarely do any of these potential tornadoes develop sufficiently to cause damage. Most of them simply pass on through or dissipate, completely unnoticed by the general public and the weather people.

You see, we at the fish camp, having been run off the lake by many approaching storms, are dedicated cloud watchers. All local disturbances receive our attention, but when a large, low, black, fast-moving cloud appears southwest of the lake, moving toward the northeast, it is time for some serious cloud watching.

Due to the unrestricted view over the lake, it is often possible to observe several little funnels forming from the base of any one large cloud. Most of these don't amount to anything—they may suddenly appear, reaching halfway to the surface, then just as rapidly disappear, moving back up into the large cloud. Some, however, are very persistent. On one occasion, we watched as a small funnel developed, then retreated to the basic cloud six times. When that particular storm cloud went out of view, the funnel was trying to form up for a seventh time and next day there were newspaper reports of damage on the beach. Undoubtedly, our little funnel touched down on its seventh try. On another occasion, ten separate funnels appeared and disappeared while one black cloud was within view. Rarely do these funnel clouds reach the ground nearby, but when this happens—

if the area is accessible—you can go there a day or two later and find evidence in the form of uprooted trees and vegetation. These twisters, since they set down in remote, uninhabited areas, receive no mention in the newspaper.

Having watched the development of normally harmless funnel clouds over the valley for years, we somewhat understand them. There are, however, two weather-related freakish occurrences that have us baffled. First, those mean-looking twisters that apparently are so minor that they pass through without being noticed by people nearby. Second, those screwy winds that occur when the sky is cloudless and there is no hint of a breeze.

George, with a passenger, was up north of the dam on his airboat when one of those small storms appeared rather suddenly. Not much of a black cloud, but still enough to get your attention. Our first thoughts were that George would spot the storm and be in before it struck. Then, as we watched, George did not come in sight, but two of those little funnel clouds suddenly appeared, dropped down, and seemed to cross the river at the dam.

The storm lasted only a short while, then all was clear. Everyone agreed that George had probably found a good location to wait it out, so we would just sit tight for a while. If he didn't show up within a reasonable period of time, we would assume he was in trouble and go looking for him.

About an hour after the storm had passed, George's airboat could be seen coming from the north. No problem now, the lake was as calm as a millpond. Arriving at the ramp, George routinely loaded his boat, and when all was secure, came inside the camp, where he was totally bewildered by the attention. Seems he had been a few miles north of the dam and had not experienced the slightest bit of bad weather. Hadn't even noticed the junior-sized tornado! Explain that one if you can—we don't even try.

Earl and I were going fishing and weather was probably our least concern. There was a small, insignificant local storm, but it didn't appear to be in our path or anywhere near our intended fishing territory. It took only a few minutes to get organized, then we were off. About two hundred yards from the camp, Earl turned around in his seat and casually mentioned that perhaps we should go back. There was no need for explanation—he simply pointed straight ahead to two small funnels, both of which were nearly touching the ground. The fishing trip could wait as we returned to the camp to watch the passing of the storm, which breezed on through, hardly noticeable. Next day though, in the marsh about four miles away, the path of a small twister was evident.

Very common, totally ignored, are the harmless-looking mini-twisters—they should probably be called whirlwinds. Normally seen from a distance, scooting across a marsh, they scatter leaves, brush, grass, and such while disturbing nothing but a few birds and insects. These are our mysterious "screwy winds," responsible no doubt, for many unexplained river events.

Duke and three other airboaters were out for a pleasant ride. The weather was ideal, not one cloud in the sky, with not even a breeze. As usual, they had chosen to go north, over the dam, and through the river run to the Oak Head. An enjoyable ride that, with side trips to the marsh, Lake Winder, and maybe the Mormon Canal, amounted to about forty miles for the round trip.

Midway through the afternoon the four returned, but Duke's boat was being towed. Now Duke always kept his boat in good shape so something unusual must have happened. Unusual indeed. Duke had sunk his boat! But how could that be? Duke was the most careful operator of the group.

As Duke explained it, he was rounding a sharp turn in the river when a sudden strange gust of wind caught his boat, causing it to partially turn over and fill with water. The other airboaters, running at one to two hundred yard intervals had not noticed any sudden gust of wind, and therefore absolutely refused to believe Duke's story of being sunk by the wind.

Let me tell you, anyone involved in a similar situation will become a believer. I personally do not doubt any part of Duke's explanation.

At the time, the mouth of Bulldozer Canal provided excellent fishing. Runoff from the marsh flushed out millions of minnows and other natural food, which, it seemed, attracted fish from far and wide. This was our private fishing hole for a considerable period of time since we obviously didn't advertise. Lazy fishing you might call it. We took along a bait bucket full of minnows, a cane pole apiece, and lawn chairs for fishing off the bank. Far different from our normal, hard-working pursuit of the biggest bass in the lake. All the different species of fish were plentiful, but this time we were after a cooler full of big fat speckled perch, which Ralph would fry so beautifully for a free fish fry at the camp. The fifteen-mile boat ride discouraged most folks, and this day we saw more huge gators than ever before or since. A tourist we talked to simply took his boat out. He would not fish a stretch of river that contained so many of these monsters. Earl and I arrived at Bulldozer, tied the boat off to some willows, took off our heavy jackets, set up the lawn chairs, and got ready for some semi-serious fishing. The fish certainly cooperated as one after another of those fat specs were deposited in the cooler. Occasionally we caught a bass of a couple pounds, the fillets of which would fry up nicely with the specs. Earl hooked a pretty darn good-sized bass, which would have been fun on a casting outfit, but proved to be no contest on a cane pole.

He accepted the ridicule graciously, then it was my turn as a thirty-pound softshell turtle latched onto my minnow. Far less of a contest than Earl's bass, the turtle simply took off in a straight line with the minnow, hook, and a good bit of my line. Earl had an excellent chance to get even, then with all that excitement out of the way, things returned to normal as we continued filling the cooler.

Earl was the first to hear a strange noise coming from the southwest. It would best be described as sounding like something mechanical. As it grew nearer and louder, apparently headed directly for our location, we speculated on what type of machine it could be. One thing for certain, it was a sound neither of us had ever before heard.

Suddenly a very strong gust of wind hit! There hadn't been even a breeze, but this brief gust was so strong, beyond a doubt it would have blown both of us off the bank and into the river had it not been for the willows we grabbed hold of. It was there and gone in an instant, leaving us completely bewildered and, once again, looking at the perfectly tranquil river run and canal.

The boat nearly blew away, our chairs and fishing poles went flying, and a heavy jacket could be seen floating in the river, against the far bank.

You could say we were still pretty confused as we retrieved the boat, collected our gear, and decided to end the fishing trip.

Back at the camp with our cooler full of fish, everyone laughed at our wild wind story. Even to this day I hesitate to repeat what happened, but one thing is for certain, if Duke tells me a sudden gust of wind tipped his airboat over, I am a believer.

More About Airboats

HIGH WATER PROVIDED ACCESS to new territories, but it also caused detours. When the river jumped up from lots of rain, airboaters found they lacked two feet of clearance for passing under the Route 192 bridge. No big deal—if they wanted to go north, they simply jumped the highway. This condition had existed for two months, but now with the water level dropping slightly each day, there would come a time when boats could once again pass under the bridge.

It was a quiet, peaceful afternoon at the camp with several people present and the normal pool game in progress. Nobody had any intentions of going riding, so Bobby, Henry's daughter, asked Larry if she could take his boat for a spin. Bobby had considerable experience running airboats and the gas tank was full so Larry said, "Sure it's ready to go."

An aircraft engine should be warmed up before it is run hard and Bobby knew this, so she fired the boat off and allowed it to idle. Then, when everything was proper, Bobby accelerated the engine some and eased off the fill into the river. But, holy mackerel! She was headed north toward the bridge, rather than south as expected.

Well, ten guys erupted from the fish camp to yell, "Don't go under the bridge!" A lot of good that did—you don't hear shouts above the noise of an airboat. As we watched, Bobby proceeded toward the bridge, not at full throttle, but going at a pretty good pace. The expected impact did not occur. She went blissfully riding under the bridge where no airboat had gone for such a long time.

One of the guys started for the bridge to warn Bobby about coming back. Too late! Here she came! Again, no problem, and Bobby was quite surprised to see the entire group awaiting her return.

Later Larry went out to check the clearance. It was less than one inch! Not much by anyone's standards, but enough to get by if there weren't any waves.

Even the most caution airboat operators are subject to an occasional revolting development. Take Dave and the newspaper people for instance.

This was to be a pleasant, leisurely tour of the river and marshes—excellent opportunities for many unusual photographs and accumulation of factual information for a special article concerning the welfare of the Upper St. Johns River. Perhaps it could be called an introduction to the marsh, though the newsmen would have preferred a less intimate introduction.

Cruising along at a reasonable speed, there were unusual sights and opportunities for pictures. Conversation was, of course, difficult, since it is nearly impossible to be heard over the noise of an airboat engine.

It was a perfectly normal outing until Dave happened upon one of the many hidden mud tussocks, which virtually stopped the boat in its tracks! The newsmen weren't holding on as well as they may have, and since an object in motion tends to stay in motion, both sailed out over the front of the boat. The boat continued moving, very slowly of course, but enough that the men could later boast that they had been run over by an airboat in the St. Johns marsh. When everything finally came to a halt, the photographer, with his equipment, was found to be half under the boat. Thankfully his head was above water with no serious damage inflicted. While that mud and muck will definitely change one's appearance, it is probably more efficient at absorbing shock and preventing injury than modern-day automobile airbags.

This particular excursion came to an abrupt conclusion while all agreed they would try it again at some later date.

Do you reckon they did?

Doggone Airboats

WHILE FISH CAMP YARNS, as a whole, require little embellishment, this is especially true concerning airboats. Many airboat accounts, in fact, defy exaggeration. With airboaters, you see, if it could happen, it did happen.

For a period of time, airboats and bulldogs seemed to go together. Call it a fad or whatever. Many felt if they owned an airboat, they should have a bulldog. Perhaps these rugged outdoorsmen felt a wild boar might be encountered at any time in the back country and where would they be without a faithful catch-dog? The fact that most of these dogs caught nothing more vicious than a biscuit didn't seem to be of any importance.

This practice, logical or not, led to numerous inevitable incidents of which the following accounts are but a small part. Anyway, with all that in mind, let me tell you about a couple of bulldogs who operated airboats.

Two old buddies were airboating down in the North Indian Field, just riding around and doing some exploring, always an enjoyable pastime. No two trips are the same. There is an ever-present possibility of something unusual and exciting around each turn. Thousands of acres of marsh, accessible only to airboats.

Now, with airboaters there is often a tendency to overestimate a boat's capabilities or, perhaps, underestimate difficult terrain. In fact, sometimes it can be attributed to bad luck. Whatever the cause, one of the riders became stuck. This was no big deal—a bit of twisting and turning usually broke the boat loose, and if that failed, someone simply got in the water and pushed. Getting stuck might warrant a bit of kidding later at the camp, but nothing more. Airboaters weren't expected to come in with clean shoes. The boat should have broken free on its own, but after some few minutes of racing the engine and working the rudders, it became apparent this was not going to happen. Time for someone to shove. The other boater, watching from his boat nearby, decided to lend a hand. He eased over the side into the shallow water, his boat with the bulldog left idling and unattended.

You couldn't blame the dog—all this activity and he wasn't included. With his master in the water shoving and the airboat motor well revved up, the bulldog naturally became excited and started jumping around. The two men, occupied with attempting to free the boat, paid no attention—until the dog jumped on the foot stand and put all his weight on the accelerator pedal!

It was definitely an attention getter when the boat went roaring off toward the east with the bulldog clinging to the foot stand, and somehow maintaining pressure on the pedal. Both of these fellows had been through a number of unusual airboat experiences, but nothing the equal of this. An airboat tearing across the shallow marsh at top speed with only a dog on board.

Nothing could be done—it was simply a matter of waiting to see what would happen next. It was some consolation that there were no obstacles in the boat's path. With a bit of luck, if the boat continued on its current course, it should ground itself somewhere in the vicinity of one lone fence post, which could be seen in the distance.

More watching and waiting for what seemed like (but certainly wasn't) a lengthy period of time. The boat, by now, was doing fifty miles an hour. Then came a startling realization—the fast-moving boat seemed to be headed toward that one lone fence post! A huge pasture field, the fence long since gone, and only one fence post remaining. As they watched in disbelief, the boat, as though guided, continued on an unswerving path, directly toward the only object that could do it harm.

Against all conceivable odds, the boat's bow did indeed center the post! The dog, of course, was thrown out and the boat, unfortunately, flopped on its side. Damage was considerable, but could have been worse. The dog, perhaps a bit bruised, was otherwise perfectly all right.

There was a lesson to be learned here: never, but never, put a bulldog in charge of an idling airboat!

Admittedly some of us are slow learners. As a result, there was a second bulldog-airboat incident that incorporated all the surprises of the first plus one more—a serious degree of danger.

It was one of those pleasant weekends, perfect for airboating, and boaters had noticeably responded. A good many boats and a large number of people, in various stages of preparation, were gathered at the camp. Some boats were in the water, some on the bank, and others were still on their trailers.

Rather peaceful actually, since the boats that were running were quietly idling. Given time, all this would change when everyone became organized and a dozen noisy boats, one by one, started roaring up the river. One of the boats, containing an extremely large bulldog, sat idling, the prop barely turning, with the bow nudged up on the bank. The owner, a considerable distance away, was visiting with friends. Interruption of the peacefulness came a little prematurely, and, you might say, could have been predicted or avoided had anyone been watching the big dog. He obediently remained in the boat, but impatient to ride, moved about from one location to another, and eventually could be seen sitting on the foot stand. All that moving about was of no consequence with the nose of the boat firmly on the bank of the river, but then—he put all his weight on the throttle pedal!

With the prop now turning at full speed, the boat had to go somewhere, and it did. First it came off the bank, reversing directions, then headed straight across the river, which at this point was about two hundred feet wide. On a straight course it was now picking up speed and appeared destined to smash into some large willows on the far bank.

The big bulldog, totally ignored up to now, had suddenly become the center of attention as everyone converged on the river bank to see what would happen next.

They, unwittingly, were in for quite a thrill. Just before reaching the willows, the boat unexpectedly reversed directions. Perhaps the dog shifted his weight and the rudders reacted. Who knows? It was now headed back toward that gathering of people and building up speed.

What had been a novel, somewhat humorous, situation now became extremely serious. It did not require a great imagination to visualize the amount of damage that could be caused by a runaway airboat charging through that throng of humanity and equipment.

People scrambled in all directions as the roaring boat closed the distance. Then, only a few feet from the river's edge, the bulldog changed positions. With his weight off the pedal, it almost appeared to have been planned. The boat obligingly idled its way back to the exact spot where it had been parked.

Beyond a doubt, this was the only successful solo roundtrip airboat ride ever achieved by a bulldog.

Uncle Billy was standing on the corner, this big old Rottweiler rubbing against his leg. Rufus, passing by, asked, "Your dog bite?"

"Heck no," replied Uncle Billy.

"Thought you said your dog wouldn't bite!" said Rufus, after bystanders had pried the dog loose from his leg.

"Ain't my dog," said Uncle Billy.

Artifacts and Indians

HOW WAS FISHING ON THE ST. JOHNS RIVER 10,000 years ago? We are not likely to find an answer to that, but evidence indicates there were fishermen back then. They just didn't bother to record their catches and pass on the information. Far different from today where we find fellows who have caught a few fish suddenly become experts, and attempting to avoid working for a living, produce how to, where to, when to, and who to books on the subject. Many old timers contend that these vast documents of fishing knowledge are worthless.

Not so with our clan, some of whom might need to start a campfire, line a birdcage, or replace the used-up Monkey Ward catalog.

Ancient Indians obviously found the banks of the river a very desirable place to live. Food was, no doubt, abundant. Fish, gators, frogs, turtles, birds, deer, and all the other land creatures that came to the river for water. Used for thousands of years as campsites, any mounds that rise above the level of the marshes will produce artifacts of one type or another. First off, these sites should not be disturbed—that is a job for professional archeologists if and when they ever get around to it. Objects found lying on the surface are interesting enough with no need for exhaustive digging.

Pottery shards and broken pieces of clay utensils are the most numerous of artifacts. With these, the variety is what makes them so interesting. Some are thick, others are extremely thin. The color may vary from red to black with all shades between.

Most are plain, but some have intricate designs and occasionally, a shard is found containing a hole. Probably a vine or something similar was used as a handle to suspend the pot over a cooking fire. The oldest of the shards are black and seem to contain fibers, possibly palmetto.

Shark's teeth are often found. Usually small, they come from species that would normally be found inshore. A few of these teeth contain holes, drilled so perfectly they appear to have been made by a drill press. Others have a slight notch in the back and it is assumed all were worn as decorations, perhaps as necklaces.

The blast from airboat props may expose hidden items. Pieces of deer antlers may be uncovered and these are usually shaped to be used as some sort of a tool. Another interesting aspect, since antlers lying on the surface would be eaten by rodents. Buried, they seem well preserved.

Flint objects are likely the most interesting items to be found. Since there is no local source for flint, this material must have been brought from distant places. The color may be white, black, gray, red, or any variations of these. With such variety in colors, the flint obviously originated from many different locations.

What may at first appear to be simply a piece of flint, upon closer examination will prove to have been a tool. Perhaps a scrapper or maybe a knife used for skinning animals. Any sizable piece of flint was used for some purpose.

An accumulation of tiny flint chips, all the same color, would indicate that long ago one of the ancients sat at that particular spot patiently shaping a spear point.

Flint spear points may be found, but are certainly not abundant. They are of various shapes and sizes. The majority are very crudely made, but occasionally there is one shaped perfectly. Using a quality reference book, most can be identified to a name, area of origin, and age. Some are though to have been in use 10,000 years ago. Fishermen of that period may have used a pole with a spear point attached.

When pieces of coquina rock are found they are usually worn smooth. The ancient Indians, no doubt, used these as we would today use sandpaper.

Bones or pieces of bones are numerous and you can only guess what type of animal they are from. Bone was apparently a handy source of material for making many things. Awls, pins, pestles, implements for weaving, and perhaps hair ornaments can be identified.

Lucky stones present a mystery. These stones, from the heads of fish, freshwater drum, have an impression of the letter "L" on one side. Sometimes carried by modern-day people as a good luck piece, what use did ancient Indians find for them?

Searching for artifacts will never replace fishing, but it is an interesting pastime while taking a break on any of the numerous mounds along the St. Johns River. What you find has no monetary value, but how many people can say they have a perfect Newnan Point or an ancient shark's tooth with two precisely drilled holes?

The ancient Indian probably worked a couple hours each day. He didn't need much—a little food, something for clothing, and some form of shelter. His primary work, now considered sport, consisted of fishing and hunting. He didn't need a car that would go 110 miles per hour, he didn't need a ten-thousand-dollar bass boat, and he didn't need air conditioning.

Modern man works forty or fifty hours a week so he can pay for a house, car, boat, clothing, food, air conditioning, etc., and if lucky, he may find a few spare hours on the weekend to go fishing or hunting. So much for progress.

Sleepless Nights

MOST FISH CAMP EVENTS were by nature short lived. The ear-splitting security alarm was a decided exception and provided week after week of hilarity, which didn't seem the least bit funny to those directly affected.

Thieves were breaking into the store at night. Such activity was, of course, against the law, but more than that, it was inconsiderate and certainly no great accomplishment, the only barrier being a latched screen door, or perhaps an unlatched window. An age-old tradition was being tampered with. No one, regardless of his honesty in other respects, should even consider breaking into the fish camp. Losses were minor and the incidents never reported. Kind of a cat and mouse game, the thieves apparently only wanting to demonstrate they could get away with it.

The break-ins could be tolerated only so long, however, and rather than set a trap for the culprits, Jane decided to purchase one of those security alarms (a horrible decision, but on with the story). Vibrations and noises activated the thing, and let me tell you, it really sounded off.

Ernie was put in charge of the device, so each night when the store was closing, he would set it up. The first few nights were uneventful—no break-ins and no alarms—but then hardly anyone knew of the alarm's presence. Tranquility was interrupted the fourth night when the machine erupted, causing everyone in the camp to turn out. Ernie, gun in hand, hustled to the store as best he could and shut the noise off, but he could find no evidence of a break-in, so he reset the alarm and returned to his cabin. This was but the first of many awakenings that were to occur over the next several weeks.

At first the alarm sounded off every two or three nights, then it was every night, and eventually two or three times each night. Ernie did the best he could, but since he had to amble about a hundred yards to the store, all the cabin residents and some neighbors down the road were wide awake before Ernie could hit the off button. There was an adjustment for sensitivity, which Ernie kept reducing, but that didn't seem to make any difference either. Believe me, folks weren't getting much sleep at night. Some started sleeping during daylight hours.

Eventually the source of the false alarms was discovered. It seems that some of the young fellows though it was fun to drive a noisy pickup near the store, race the engine a little, then take off before being seen. Nighttime airboaters, purposely or accidentally, also contributed.

After countless sleepless nights, it was now obvious—the security alarm would not solve the original problem. Ernie turned it off and resorted to a more direct approach. Since he wasn't getting any sleep anyway, why not just stand watch all night? Results were almost immediate when he interrupted a break-in and fired a couple warning shots. There were stolen cans of beer strewn out the driveway and down the road, but the problem had been solved. There would be no more break-ins.

Next day, the infernal machine was unhooked and retired, never to be seen again. Nighttime peacefulness was restored, and within days people had caught up on their sleep.

Contests

COMMON, EVERYDAY, RUN-OF-THE-MILL CONTESTS aren't too interesting to anyone except the participants. Pool games, horseshoes, fishing, darts—all these have their winners who are almost immediately forgotten. The winners are normally displaced next month, next week, next day, or even next game. Unusual contests, on the other hand, produce winners who are remembered for years to come. Indeed, if the competition is conducted only once, the champion remains forever.

Take the spontaneous corn-eating contest. Actually, when all except one of the contestants dropped out early in the competition, it became more of an endurance contest.

The Conservation Club, sponsoring one of its big free feeds, had an abundance of that mouth-watering Zellwood sweet corn. Undeniably the best sweet corn ever produced—and since this had been prepared by Ernie, it was indeed the best of the best.

With all that super corn available, someone brought up a question. How many ears could a person eat? This, quite naturally, led to some eating and counting. Very innocent to start with, then a few corn eaters became more serious. The count hadn't yet reached impressive numbers when one by one the competitors chose to withdraw. George was solely responsible. Whenever anyone established a number, he exceeded it by one. All the others were obviously over matched. While they struggled, George consumed each ear as though it was his first. Inevitably, George, still eating corn, was declared the winner.

It could have, should have, would have ended at this point

except for one of our many agitators. He insisted that George was still just cruising and we hadn't yet answered the original question—how much Zellwood sweet corn can a person eat? No objections from George, he was game, so the count went on. Now with his former competitors acting as cheerleaders, George began struggling at a count of thirty-five. He wouldn't quit, though, until he reached thirty-seven ears.

Now that may or may not be a state, national, or world record. Who knows? One thing is for certain, since both the fish camp and the Conservation Club are now extinct, it is a local record that stands little chance of ever being surpassed.

We might just mention that George was off his feed for the next couple of days—a small price to pay for earning the title of Lake Washington Corn-Eating Champ!

There was another contest that George may very well have won, had our entry form not been rejected. Some thoughtful group over on the beach sponsored what they called the Ugly Bartender Contest. George, helping part time at the camp, should have been eligible to compete. So we, with a great deal of confidence, sent in the required photo and completed entry form. Our entry was returned—George was not eligible.

Apparently those high-class folks on the beach felt they would be severely overmatched in competition with us river rats.

I stopped by the fish camp this particular morning and found all the doors and windows open. Obviously, that worthless air conditioner was, once again, not working.

Now there are three things I disapprove of in a fish camp. One is air conditioning, another is a noisy juke box, and the third is tipping the beer tender. Folks who want perfect comfort and the opportunity to pay extra for a bottle of beer while having their hearing destroyed should patronize one of those watering holes uptown.

Anyway, with the doors and windows open and no screens, the place was full of flies. Not just a few, mind you, there were swarms of those pests. Everyone seemed to be taking the invasion in stride. No complaints were voiced even though each person kept one hand, sometimes both hands, busy, brushing the insects away from their beer. I suggested we appoint a scorekeeper, pass the fly swatter around, and have a fly swatting contest. We could promote a friendly sporting event and rid the place of flies in the process. Due, no doubt, to pure laziness, my proposal was turned down. Then, on top of that, an insult. Ralph casually mentioned that there hadn't been any fly problem until I showed up, and me fresh out of the shower.

Stu arrived, repaired the air conditioner in short order, and closed the doors and windows. As I was leaving, one of those who professed there was no fly problem told Stu, "Put that thing down on freezing! Maybe it will immobilize these darned flies that are driving us nuts!"

What's this world coming to when people are so lazy they won't swat a fly?

Our peanut-throwing contest was billed as a world championship event since the Guinness Book of World Records contained no reference to peanut throwing. The rules were simple—contestants were required to throw uphill, against the wind, and through the trees. All thrown peanuts were to remain where they fell for the benefit of the local squirrel population.

Not that any of our honest, upstanding participants would cheat, peanut throwing is an event that requires close scrutiny. It is common knowledge that a peanut loaded with buckshot can be thrown a country mile.

Competition was brisk right from the start and the boys with the tape were busy measuring each throw and announcing the distance. The squirrels were equally busy and when one swiped an unmeasured peanut, the contestant was awarded a free throw.

With no outstanding leader, the competition had continued for quite some time when Stan The Man cut loose with a toss that seemed to get caught in an updraft. That peanut sailed and sailed until it finally came to rest on the canal bank. Had it gone farther, the measuring crew would have had to go swimming. The tape indicated 187 feet, and this definitely deflated all of Stan's competition.

A few more throws were made, including one that looked very good until it became hung up in the top of a persimmon tree, then all the competitors dropped out and Stan was declared "World Champion Peanut Thrower."

It is totally unimportant and probably shouldn't even be mentioned, but the measurements may not have been completely accurate. The only tape we could locate had been discarded by a construction crew when several feet broke off the end.

Now to call Stan The Man a professional peanut thrower would be unfair. We can say, however, he was raised in peanut country and has thrown more peanuts than most folks have eaten.

We were getting primed for a big-time roach race when an informant passed word that one of the participating bugs was on steroids. Since we had no means of testing for drugs, the contest was called off.

You know those big apple snails, which abound in our local

fresh waters, a favorite food of the Everglades kite and limpkin? We rounded up a bunch of those rascals and painted little numbers on their shells in preparation for a snail race. What a disappointment. When we dumped them in the center of a circular arena, they all became romantic. This race was called off due to lack of interest on the part of the racers.

Someone asked about a frog-jumping contest, but with the fondness these folks have for frog legs, it is impossible to assemble enough frogs for competition.

Hogs

THIS BRIEF AND (I HOPE) EDUCATIONAL DISCUSSION does not relate to 1) Arkansas' outstanding football team; 2) those guys who attempt to bankrupt an all-you-can-eat restaurant; or 3) your luxurious, gas-consuming car. No, we're going to stick with those four-legged rooters that hang around the edge of the St. Johns River marsh, minding their own business and trying to stay out of the sights of our mighty hunters.

Hereabouts, hogs were introduced by early Spanish explorers. Perhaps some escaped confinement or were purposely released into the wild. Whatever. When they became established, this certainly must have pleased the panthers, bears, and, last but not least, the remaining Indians.

Anyone familiar with only domestic hogs might feel that hogs would have little chance in the wild, but, in fact, the wild hog does very well. Extremely prolific and having few natural enemies, today's hogs would overrun territories if their population weren't kept in check by hunting and trapping. Even so, there are often reports of a momma hog and her piglets in the suburbs.

What happens to trapped hogs? Well, some are converted to pork while others are sold to game farms, where they are released to be pursued by "gentlemen" hunters. These mighty hog hunters pay a sizable fee, climb into a vehicle and are driven around to select and bag their porker. Hunting clothing is optional; a business suit and tie will suffice since these sportsmen are not expected to get even the slightest bit dirty.

We once had a huge population of wild hogs roaming the St. Johns River valley. No great attraction. A few were shot and converted to meat; some were caught to be pen raised and fattened. One of the good old boys found that he could sell wild hogs at some of the local watering holes for $30 apiece, and he was often seen coming in with four or five in the bottom of his boat. Jeff and Ronnie Hillpot tried a hand at this business, which was perfectly all right except on those evenings when they weren't able to sell their hogs and had hot dates, and I would find myself cleaning hogs at 11:00 p.M. by the lights of the carport.

Wild hogs have an uncanny ability to simply vanish from sight. In cover that would barely hide a rabbit, now you see them, now you don't. Once, two young lads saw a herd (flock? covey? gaggle?) of wild hogs at the end of Sarno Road and were going home for a gun. They came charging in off the lake, their outboard running at full speed, tied the boat up, and hurried to their truck.

No point in trying to discourage them. They broke every speed limit between the camp and their house and were soon back with a shotgun and a full box of shells. Off again with the spray flying. Now, the predictable outcome. They returned eventually—wet, muddy, tired, disappointed, and disgusted. Given a little cover, wild hogs will disappear while you watch. Don't leave expecting them to await your return.

Some old-timers may remember several years ago when a large, totally white hog was often seen north of Lake Washington. Stories of the ghost hog circulated for two full years and, to the best of my knowledge, no one ever bagged that admirably elusive creature.

Ronnie once brought Henry four little pigs. Poor judgment, of course, but they were easy to catch and kinda cute. Now, if you're going to keep pigs, you need a pen, something Ronnie had not considered until he spent the remainder of the day following Henry's instructions regarding how and where it should be built.

I visited the pig pen only once; didn't linger long but learned a lasting lesson. Among other things, wild hogs are host to millions of fleas, a fact that recalls to memory another humorous wild hog escapade.

Two of the good old boys, Camp Holly regulars, decided they needed some hog meat and set off up the river with a twenty-two rifle and a somewhat unreliable outboard motor. About ten miles away was a hog-infested area where you could shoot a hog near the river and not have to drag it very far. They whiled away most of the afternoon just sitting in the boat and also bagged three good-sized hogs within easy dragging distance. With an occasional pull from the jug of shine they carried, time passed quickly. It was indeed an enjoyable and profitable outing.

Realizing it would be dark before long, they field-dressed the three hogs, threw them into the bottom of the boat, and were ready to head home. However, the sorry motor would not start! Now let me tell you, walking out of the St. Johns River marsh ain't no piece of cake. In some locations it's downright impossible. Of course, they tinkered with the motor a little between pulls on the jug, then, with the coming of complete darkness, said to heck with it and curled up in the bottom of the boat.

Now, a bit of educational information for those who have never had an opportunity to be involved in such a situation. Parasitic insects such as fleas, ticks, and lice tend to leave a cooling carcass and seek a live, warm host. Consequently, our two boys awoke to find they had problems that even the jug of shine would not cure. You will probably agree that they were due for a little good luck, and, thankfully, the motor now started on the first yank.

Butchering the hogs could wait. It took three baths each before they were rid of all the hitchhikers. Liberal application of what remained in the jug provided a pretty good antiseptic and, so far as the hunters were concerned, assurance they would not develop tick fever or brucellosis.

It may just be my imagination, but people don't seem to have fun like that anymore. And, oh, yes, after much research, consultation with knowledgeable authorities, and other such homework, I now know what a group of wild hogs is called: a sounder! I'll just leave that important bit of information with you for whatever it's worth.

Uh-Oh

YOU KNOW, THERE IS ABSOLUTELY NO REASON to become upset and excited over some unfortunate event that has already occurred. Too late to prevent it. Just accept the outcome, keep cool, smile, and vow that such a thing will never again happen. Profound advice for others, but we old swamp rats will normally continue to fuss, cuss, and remain irritable long after the incident has occurred.

There is no limit to the number of things that can go wrong during a planned fishing trip, hunting trip, or something as simple as a boat ride. Pleasant things also happen, but, what the heck, they're expected.

Reports of huge bass being caught in the Stick Marsh prompted Bubba and Hank to get in on the action. On Saturday morning they would leave the house early enough to be among the first at the launch ramp. They would use Bubba's boat but Hank would have to drive since Bubba's wife had taken the car to visit relatives.

Friday evening found them making final preparations. Beer was iced; shiners were put into the live well with the aerator running; the boat's tank was filled with gas; and sardines, Vienna sausages, and crackers were gathered for snacks. Nothing had been overlooked.

It was 4:00 A.M. Any earlier and they might just as well have not gone to bed at all. The truck was backed up to hook up the boat, and—guess what? The boat trailer had a one-and-three-quarter-inch hitch and the truck had a two-inch ball! Bubba and

Hank weren't going anywhere, and with a start like that they may as well have gone back to bed.

Though I witnessed it only once, you can be certain the following fiasco is reenacted each year at various locations around Florida. It was not yet daylight and boats were lining up, ready to launch. Eager and anxious fishermen were everywhere, all definitely in a hurry to get started. Here comes the game warden, a nice guy who is giving everyone a break. This is the first day a new fishing license is required; if he checks you at the ramp, he won't have to give you a citation later. You don't have a new license? Well, the county license bureau is only seventeen miles away and they open at 8:00 A.M.

Admittedly, boat plugs are a necessity. Even so, they have been known to cause problems. Conversely, absence of a boat plug, under various circumstances, might also result in embarrassment.

You pull into the yard after a successful fishing trip, unhook the trailer in its customary parking spot, and prop up the tongue. Everything is fine until three days later, when we have one of those toad-strangling rains. You first notice the trailer tires are flat; then, of course, you find the boat contains a few hundred gallons of rainwater. The problem, old buddy, is definitely a boat plug.

Two old boys weren't even going fishing; they were taking a couple of the kids out to learn water skiing. They launched the boat, tied it off, parked the car and trailer, then went inside the camp for a beer. It was a hot, sweltering day, and that first beer tasted so good, they had another. Actually, they were on their third beer when the boys entered to inform them that the boat was on the bottom of the lake. Problem? This time an absent boat plug.

Yet another blunder: it was early morning, still dark, and Richard was fixin' to go fishin'. He had parked the boat, motor, and trailer in the side yard and, due to occasional thievery, had taken the precaution of chaining the motor to a convenient tree. Hooking the trailer to the truck, even in the dark, was no problem. Then he was off down the bumpy road headed for Blue Cypress Lake. About thirty minutes and twenty miles later, it became light enough to see. Would you believe? There was no boat on the trailer! Yes, sir, that chain had done its job. The boat and motor were still secure in the side yard.

Oftentimes there is no substitute for experience. The water was extremely low so, as usual, the old boat ramp was hard to use. We regulars didn't consider it a problem and had lived with it for years. Inexperienced newcomers, however, didn't seem to realize that in order to have traction on your rear wheels, you must have weight on them. Sometimes the solution was as simple as having someone stand on the back bumper. The following account illustrates an even more simple solution.

A couple of fellows, evidently new to airboating since none of us recognized them, had been out riding and were now back, loading their boat. To the loafers in the fish camp, the first indication of their ignorance was the squealing of tires. Now, this group was not hard-hearted or uncaring; they felt if the guy with the problem figured it out for himself, it would have a more lasting effect. Well, the tires squealed, then silence. More squealing, more silence. Continued squealing interrupted by periods of silence until it began to get on everyone's nerves. Don got up, moved to where he could analyze the situation, muttered a few choice cuss words, then ambled off toward the ramp. The rest, now taking a little interest, got up to watch. Don, rather irritated, could be seen giving instructions to the driver, then, walking on the trailer to avoid getting his feet wet, he climbed into the boat. Next thing you know, he fired off the airboat and shoved the entire rig out of the water and up the incline. With the car, boat, and trailer now sitting on level pavement, he shut the engine off, crawled out of the boat, and returned to the camp without saying a word.

School was out. Don returned to his beer. And the lesson of the day was probably impressive.

Buckyboar

THE JACKALOPE OF THE SOUTHWEST, deserving or not, has attracted a great deal of attention and gained notoriety beyond belief. That's certainly OK with us old river rats, but, then again, why should anyone become excited over such a puny little critter? Shucks, we have insects as unusual and noteworthy as the jackalope. Take the indestructible cow ant, for instance. Frustrated in his attempts to stomp one, my friend Larry fired seven rounds from his 8mm handgun. When last seen, the ant was continuing on to its destination, and, though opinions vary, most feel Larry simply didn't have enough firepower.

Anyway, it is highly unlikely the jackalope could survive hereabouts. Quite some number of years back, the state imported and released a small herd of antelope, a cousin of the jackalope. An unsuccessful venture, to say the least. Constant aerial surveys of the herd found their numbers decreasing daily. Now, frankly, central Florida does not appear to be ideal habitat for pronghorns, but, then again, many old-timers living out there in the woods had never had an opportunity to sample antelope steaks. Whatever the reason, as mentioned, the antelope stocking program was no howling success.

When it comes to establishing a desirable species, the outcome is normally a failure, while the reverse is predictably true with exotic undesirable species. We have walking catfish, armored catfish, tilapia, fire ants, and others not yet well publicized. It seems that customs passes everything except piranha, and once a species is approved for import, it will most certainly become established. If Grandma Ledbetter had piranha in her aquarium and they became a problem, she wouldn't want to kill the rascals. Heck, no, they're pets! So, quite naturally, they would be dumped into a nearby ditch.

With all that out of the way, let me tell you about Bill. You see, Bill was kind of a hermit whose home was a shack built among that small stand of cypress trees on the far southern end of Lake Hellen Blazes. Anyone bothering to look would find traces of his shack today. Living in the marsh, Bill observed many unusual things others were not privileged to see. Take the Skunk Ape, for instance. We read modern-day newspaper accounts concerning sightings of this large, hairy, obnoxious-smelling, manlike creature, most likely originating from the Everglades or the Okefenokee Swamp. Bill insisted he had once heard, smelled, and caught a glimpse of this legendary creature off a slough in the river. Now, I myself have encountered some overripe bass fishermen who, having found some terrific fishing, couldn't tear themselves away to shave or shower. Bill didn't feel these qualified as Skunk Apes.

Not really much of a talker, Bill once told me briefly of a strange critter he had caught and raised as a pet. He gave no details whatsoever, only that his unusual pet had expired at the age of three and he had had it mounted. My introduction to Buckyboar was sudden and brief. Bill had decided to return to civilization and was taking off for parts unknown. Everything he possessed could be worn or carried with one exception: his mounted pet! Would I take care of Buckyboar and, if possible, keep his existence a secret? This wasn't really much to ask of a friend so, under cover of darkness, we switched Bucky from Bill's boat to my pickup.

Bill hasn't been seen in a coon's age and Old Bucky has become a bit tattered and shabby, but it seems time to bring him out of hiding. Buckyboar now hangs on the wall as a reminder of Bill and the many mysteries of the St. Johns River marsh. (See photo page 101.)

Good Eatin' Fish

HOW ABOUT A BRIEF DISSERTATION regarding the eating qualities of fish caught in our local St. Johns River system? There have been many heated fish camp debates about which variety is the best, but perhaps that is simply a matter of personal preference. It is safe to say that all of our native fish can be eaten, and I for one have tried them all.

Let's consider the lowly mudfish, for example. This prehistoric fish goes by many names, and if he chews up your favorite bass lure, you may call him names we are not going to quote here. The accepted official name appears to be bowfin, but the fish may also be known as cypress trout, grennel, dogfish, and cottonfish, its Indian name. Regardless of what you call it, this fish is recommended for eating only when you are desperately hungry and have absolutely nothing else to eat. Charlie Wilson was known to clean and cook mudfish, then serve it to whoever happened to be present as proof the fish could be eaten. With the method Charlie employed—a very small piece of fish quite thoroughly covered with a thick, highly seasoned batter—perhaps anything nonpoisonous could have been substituted. Stranger things have happened, but don't expect blackened mudfish to become featured at classic seafood establishments.

Dave Pinyerd, my old fishing buddy, had a cat that dearly loved fish. Over the years, we learned to trust the cat's opinion. When we filleted a mudfish, cut it into small pieces, and placed it in the cat's bowl, the cat approached the bowl, took one sniff, and walked out of the kitchen. Now, friends, everyone to his own opinion, but I don't want to eat any fish a cat won't touch.

How about gar? Have you ever eaten gar fish? If your answer is no, you may have eaten it without knowing. George Saad, a friend of several years back, owned a small diner that had quite a reputation for its delicious fish sandwiches. Some years after George sold the diner, he confided in me that his fish sandwiches were gar tail. He used only that part behind the anal fin, which produced two nice sandwich-size fillets. Gar tail fish sandwiches, certainly not advertised as such, will be found only where gar are plentiful, easy to catch, and, consequently, inexpensive.

Jackfish, as it's called locally, is another fish with several names. If you are going to enter one in a fishing contest, best you call it an eastern chain pickerel, but it is often called pike or just plain pickerel too. Since this is an extremely bony fish, few people bother to clean it. The flesh of the jackfish may, however, be the sweetest and best of all our fishes. It can be filleted and all the bones removed, but, friends, that is an undertaking. It may also be filleted to remove the large bones, then ground and made into patties. I once encountered a lakeside fish camp restaurant that served fish sandwiches made with jackfish patties. It was common for people to drive thirty or forty miles to this particular restaurant just to eat this specialty. The proprietor never had to purchase any fish; people fishing out of the camp always gave him what jackfish they caught rather than go to the trouble of cleaning them. The first choice of Dave's cat, the fish connoisseur, was jackfish. When we brought him other varieties, he might get mildly excited, but when we had jackfish, he somehow knew even before the cooler was opened. Just put the fish on a piece of newspaper and step aside; the cat took over from there.

Mullet are saltwater fish that sometimes venture into fresh water. At times, Lake Washington contained impressive schools of large mullet. It is humorous when visiting fishermen mistake them for a school of large bass, but that is another story. Determined to check the eating qualities of mullet from Lake

Washington, I snagged three and prepared them for the skillet. The fillets looked good enough but seemed to have an extremely fishy odor. I should have stopped at this point, but live and learn. When the fish started cooking, everyone in the house—and maybe some of the neighbors—complained. It was a lost cause. The flavor seemed to match the odor. A couple of bites proved they could be eaten. Then I had to air the house out and carry the remains to the marsh for the gators.

We have suckers in local waters (not to be confused with those humans who, upon becoming mesmerized by TV fishing shows and lure demonstrations, fill their tackle boxes with expensive, seldom-used ornaments). Suckers (the fish) are not plentiful and you are not likely to catch any. However, they're good eating even if they're rather bony.

Before the devastating 1990 fish kill, Lake Washington was absolutely loaded with huge channel catfish. Many of us expected the state record to be beaten by a fish from Lake Washington. John Rawley came close, and there was a story that a visiting couple did actually beat the record but failed to register the fish. The population and size of these fish, unbelievable to others, could be appreciated only by the few of us who took time to survey results of the fish kill. Truckloads of dead channel catfish—ten, fifteen, twenty, thirty pounds and more—washed against the lake and river banks to be harvested by gators, buzzards, and other scavengers. Anyway, those huge catfish were easy to clean and excellent eating. The inferior belly meat was discarded and the fillets cut into smaller pieces for easier cooking. One fish would make a meal for several people. All other species of catfish are equally good eating, though there's more work cleaning and less meat for the skillet.

Bream is a name often applied to nearly all members of the sunfish family. Serious bream fishermen, however, make a distinction among bluegill, pumpkinseed, longear sunfish, redbreast sunfish, shellcracker, stumpknocker, and warmouth. All are excellent eating. Dedicated bream fishermen are quite happy that, because of the fish's normally small size, many anglers do not fish for bream. This means more fish for the true bream fishermen.

What can be said about speckled perch? It's favorite fishing for many folks, and no one can dispute the eating qualities. Crappie is probably the most accepted name, though it may be called calico bass and locally is just plain spec. Under other than impossible conditions, all expert spec fishermen will catch fish. Our local specs, generally speaking, are larger than most. There have been times when a catch of specs averaged more than a pound and nearly a pound and a half. A poll of fishermen would probably name specs as our best-eating fish. As for my personal opinion, I can only say that Dave's cat was never given an opportunity to sample specs.

Bass, the most popular of all our fish, are sought for their legendary fighting ability and willingness to strike artificial lures. The popularity of bass fishing has created various theories regarding harvesting of the fish. Some feel all bass should be released; others feel harvesting for food has little detrimental effect on the population. Actually, without going too deeply into this controversy, releasing or keeping bass should depend upon many factors too numerous to mention. Bass are good eating fish—perhaps not the best but still fine eating. Smaller bass are preferred by most people, and skinning is recommended.

In the mid-1960s I became acquainted with an old gentleman who was then in his late seventies. Some younger folks would occasionally take the old fellow along when they went fishing out of Camp Holly. He had lived in Melbourne his entire life and had fished the St. Johns River since boyhood. Delightful to talk to, he explained that he now fished for fun, though years back he fished for food. He still kept, cleaned, and ate what he caught even though he had plenty of other things to eat. When asked if he caught many big bass years ago, he described what was probably a periodic excursion to the river.

The entire family would participate. Leaving Melbourne early in the day, they would walk the Union Cypress Railroad to the trestle. Shiners were plentiful and were used as bass bait. Apparently much of their fishing was done by sight and they always fished for the biggest bass. He described how they searched until they spotted a big one, then dropped a shiner in front of it. The bass invariably took the shiner and was landed. The family fished virtually the entire day, then trudged back to Melbourne carrying a number of six- to ten-pound bass.

Allowing a bit for exaggeration, I can still visualize the family group walking the Union Cypress Railroad late in the day, each member with a cane pole over one shoulder and a string of large bass over the other.

Ladies Handbags

WHAT DOES AN OLD RIVER RAT KNOW about ladies handbags? Virtually nothing, but the same can be said about many other top-secret subjects.

Our bank has a notice posted on the front door that says, "For security purposes, the following items may not be worn beyond this point." Would you believe that fishing caps are on the list? Now, to the best of my knowledge, the only thing that can be hidden under a fishing cap is a bald head. Ladies handbags are not listed but any fool should realize a ladies handbag might contain an arsenal. (Discrimination against fishermen, I guess, but actually the security aspect doesn't bother me in the slightest since I only visit the bank once each month to cash my dole check. The check is so small, the clerks can almost take care of it from the change drawer.)

Your tackle box may be the largest manufactured and it may contain every imaginable item needed for a two-week fishing vacation. Old buddy, that box is very impressive, but when the truck breaks down or the outboard motor won't start, don't give up until you've checked your wife's handbag. That needed repair item may be nestled there among an inventory of ten thousand other objects.

Henry had obtained two tickets to the Alabama-Florida football game in Gainesville back when booze was a bigger issue than the game itself. There would absolutely be no intoxicating beverages allowed in the stadium. It made little difference to the two of us. But when the newspapers created such a big deal of it, the proclamation became a challenge. Game day found us passing through the gate, each carrying a pint of cheap hooch cleverly concealed inside our folded parkas. Quite proud of ourselves, we found our seats to be much better than expected—second row from the field. The entire row ahead of us remained vacant until kick-off time. Then here came a large group of folks, all Alabama fans like Henry and I.

These folks were serious football fans. They had arrived before noon in three motor homes, parked in the allotted area, and started their pre-game tailgate party on schedule. Kick-off time somewhat disrupted their festivities so they stowed the food, assembled their portable bar, and joined thousands of others in the stadium. Two of the ladies carried handbags so enormous they should have had wheels and tow straps. Darndest thing you ever saw when they set up the bar between the two rows of seats. They had top-shelf liquors of all types, a variety of mixes, glasses, ice cubes, and even swizzle sticks. When they were finished, you almost expected them to erect a neon sign announcing the bar was open for business.

Let me tell you, it was party time! Gator and Crimson Tide fans alike were served. Everyone was welcome, including the security guards. The outcome of the game lost importance as time went by, and Alabama's loss on the basis of a couple of fluke field goals didn't make a bit of difference. No hard feelings; wait till next year.

So much for the no-booze-in-the-stadium proclamation.

Now to the incident that brought up the subject of handbags. This couple (names unknown, of course) were out for an airboat ride. They had previously discussed the merits of adding a small gator to their well-populated pond. They already had a variety of fish, a couple of soft-shelled turtles, and plenty of visiting wading birds. Why not a small gator to make the setting complete?

You might say the young lady was somewhat experienced in handling gators. Easing through a slough, there was a small gator right alongside the boat. So, quite naturally, she grabbed the little fellow for closer examination. Nope, this one was too large, maybe three feet. She innocently turned to show it to her companion, who was genuinely impressed as he shouted, "Get that %#$*@!#* thing away from me and get it out of the boat!" As the young lady eased the little gator back into the water, she made one comment that I hope doesn't attract the attention of the game warden.

"It wouldn't have fit in my handbag anyway."

Autopilots and Self-Starters

I WAS GOING TO WORK AT MY USUAL EARLY HOUR—not many awake and darned few lights on in the neighborhood. Maybe a block from the house, something caught my attention. A car that had been parked on a slightly inclined driveway was backing out into my path. It had no lights on and was moving so slowly you could hardly detect it was moving at all. Curious about what kind of dummy was driving, I stopped. With the wheels slightly cramped, that car backed ever so slowly into the street and parked itself neatly against the right-hand curb. There was no one in or near the vehicle.

You may have heard of an airboat starting by itself: no one near it; the boat just cranked up. Well, folks, that's a slight exaggeration. The boat never actually started. Honest facts about airboats are sometimes hard to swallow. Let's not overdo it.

What would you have done? It's midnight, you've had a hard day out on the river, it's raining outside, and you're sleeping soundly when you hear your airboat, not far from the bedroom window, cranking away and fixing to start! You would probably do what Pop Fortenberry did: jump out of bed, put on a pair of shoes, grab your famous old wire-and-tape-wrapped shotgun, and dash out into the rain! (Incidentally, a gun doesn't have to be pretty to shoot straight.) Some dirty low-life varmint was trying to steal his boat!

A little cold rain tends to wake a person rather rapidly. Pop found himself getting soaked with nothing and nobody to shoot at. No, sir, nothing whatsoever in sight except the boat with the prop turning over just as nice as you please, making every effort to start, but the mag switches were off. Wide awake now, Pop realized the rain had shorted out the starter switch. He would have to disconnect the battery. No real harm done. Pop was soaked and cold, and a few neighbors had been awakened. But, what the heck, it was all part of the fun of owning an airboat.

After that, when Jane Fortenberry had relatives or friends overnight, she always took the precaution of telling them, "If you hear an airboat running through the yard in the middle of the night, think nothing of it."

Pop, the Hunter

POP, *A FRIEND OF MANY YEARS BACK,* was a darned nice guy and enjoyable to be around—most of the time. Come hunting season, however, Pop was to be avoided. There didn't appear to be any logical explanation, but when it came to hunting, Pop was a walking disaster looking for some place to happen. Pop's consistent failures at hunting eventually became accepted as routine, so only his more bizarre encounters remain well remembered.

Long before the season opened one year, Pop had obtained permission to hunt a rather choice piece of farmland. Opening day found Pop, by himself, entering a forty-acre pasture that contained only one cow and one tree. Absolutely no way to get into any trouble under such conditions. But just as Pop reached the tree, the cow seemed to become irritated and charged. Had he mistaken a bull for a cow? Nope, it was a cow, all right, but she was sure acting like a mad bull. Pop circled the tree a couple of times with the cow on his heels, then grabbed a lower branch and pulled himself up out of harm's way. Expecting the cow to leave, he made himself comfortable on a branch and waited. As Pop explained it later, the cow became more infuriated, charging around and around the tree, pawing up dirt and bellowing something fierce! Pop claimed this went on for an hour. Then the cow suddenly stopped, stiffened up, and fell dead!

Well, Pop could now get out of the tree, but he still had a problem. Fully expecting the farmer to demand payment for the cow, he went to the farmhouse, found the farmer and tried to explain. The cow was dead, but he hadn't fired a shot. Noting Pop's anxiety, the farmer couldn't resist feigning a show of serious anger. Then with visions of Pop dashing around the tree, the cow on his heels, the farmer burst into laughter. For some unknown reason, the cow had been acting very strangely and had been separated from the herd. Under such humorous conditions, he could accept loss of the cow.

Pop could also laugh now, but he wasn't laughing while the cow chased him around the tree.

The same farm had a small pond that, during duck season, often held a few migrating ducks. Early one morning, Pop very quietly slipped through the brush and surprised six mallards, which took off with the usual flurry of wings, splashing water, and a couple of squawks. Pop blazed away with his twelve-gauge and managed to bag one duck, which fell lifeless in the center of the pond. Maybe he should have gotten two or three, but Pop was happy with one.

Now he had a problem he had not anticipated. How would he get the duck? Pop sat down on a convenient log, figuring the duck would eventually drift to the edge of the pond. After a while, however, with no breeze, his duck remained where it had fallen. Now, quite frankly, Pop seldom bagged any ducks or, for that matter, anything else. He was not going to abandon this prize.

Nearly desperate enough to doff his clothes and swim to the duck, he noticed a tiny decrepit wooden boat pulled up on the bank. It didn't look as though it had been used in years and the bottom leaked badly, but, Pop reasoned, if he was extremely careful, it would float long enough to retrieve his bird. He found a board for a paddle and crawled in with his shotgun. With very little of the boat above water, Pop located his duck, tossed it into the boat, and turned for shore. Well, he had almost made it when the bottom fell out and the boat fell apart! Pop grabbed his gun and the duck as he settled feet first to the bottom! There he was, up to his chin in cold water, the gun held high with one hand and his precious duck in the other. Pop waded out and didn't waste any time getting to his car, then home for a hot shower.

This would not have been a typical hunting trip for anyone other than Pop.

Here's one more of Pop's hunting misadventures. Long before the arrival of duck season, an announcement was made. Applications could be submitted for a special hunt to be conducted in an area of marsh historically accepted as the best in the state. Many thousands of applicants were anticipated, and the few allotted winners would be chosen by a random drawing. This was a once-in-a-lifetime opportunity at absolutely no expense. Just get yourself to a specified location on a specified day at a specified time with your hunting equipment.

Like many others, Pop submitted an application but with little confidence. A full month passed and Pop had completely forgotten about his application when his wife called him at work with the good news: he was a winner! No more work accomplished that day—Pop was busy informing all his cronies of his good fortune. Perhaps Pop's hunting luck was changing for the better. Why he chose Virgil as his hunting partner remains a mystery, but without Virgil we would have no story.

Hunting in this area was so good there could be no excuse for even a rank amateur not to get his limit. With plenty of time to prepare, Pop and Virgil made their plans and went over every detail almost daily. Both would set their alarms, and the first one up would call the other to make certain he was up. Pop would drive and have a full tank of gas. Virgil would buy the ammunition: three boxes, seventy-five rounds. They shouldn't need nearly that much but were taking no chances. Each would bring a dozen decoys, and they would leave in time to arrive at their destination one hour early. They had everything but a checklist; as things developed, that would have been no help anyway.

The special morning arrived, both alarms went off, the phone call was made, and before long Pop arrived at Virgil's house. Everything was rechecked: shotguns, ammunition, decoys, sandwiches and coffee. Nothing was left to chance.

On schedule, everything continued in perfect order. They checked in an hour early and were shown their assigned rowboat, into which they loaded and rechecked each item. Precisely on time the powerboat started, and they were towed the four miles to their blind. With plenty of time before sunrise, they set out their decoys in a pattern previously agreed upon, then hid the boat and took their seats in the blind.

Maybe fifteen minutes before shooting time, Virgil handed Pop a box of shells. Pop opened the box and, though it was not yet light enough to see clearly, had a sudden feeling of despair. The flashlight verified his worst nightmare: three boxes of sixteen-gauge shells for two twelve-gauge shotguns! Everything and everyone on the marsh received an early wake-up call when Pop blew his top!

Virgil may have been speechless but Pop made up for that. "You dumb #(P@O/.#*! Here are the car keys. Get your butt in that boat and don't come back without shells that fit my gun!" Well, away went Virgil, who, with little rowing experience, wasn't doing too well. He did, however, manage to stir up a few ducks and irritate several duck hunters. Pop, with nothing else to do, drank coffee and watched the many ducks that landed among their decoys. Here was an excellent opportunity to observe undisturbed duck behavior, but Pop didn't exactly take advantage of it.

Virgil made pretty good time. He returned after about five hours with a box of twelve-gauge shells, but he was exhausted and had lost all interest in duck hunting. Not having noticed that shooting in the marsh had ended, Pop eagerly loaded his shotgun. But the ducks had gone to open water, where they would not be bothered. They would return about twilight.

As you might imagine, there was little conversation in the blind, during the short boat ride, or during the drive home.

Bites

NOW, SOMETIME WHEN YOU ARE JUST SITTING AROUND with a bunch of the boys and all subjects of interest have seemingly been used up, casually mention the effects of some unusual bite. Of course, there will be some who stray from the subject and include stings; that's permissible and accepted within reason. Some city boys simply don't know what bites and what stings, and, of course, most bites sting anyway. Well, friend, you're in for a couple of hours of competitive conversation. Everyone has been bitten by something or other, and with the normal amount of exaggeration some of these accounts become classics. (By the way, stories of being bitten by the love bug will not be tolerated; everyone should know that our locally abundant love bugs neither bite nor sting.)

With all that out of the way, let me tell you about Dave's encounter with the oyster fish. That may not be the fish's scientific name, but he has earned it by cracking oyster shells. This was a little fellow, maybe eight inches long and harmless looking. Dave certainly didn't want the fish; he did, however, want his hook back to save re-rigging, and that hook was buried in a mighty tough little jaw. Should be no problem. With bass, we just stuck a thumb in its mouth to hold it open while shaking the hook free. Apparently that method didn't work so well since Dave, who didn't use much profanity, scorched the ears of everyone within hearing. I personally thought it was kind of funny when I turned and saw Dave shaking the heck out of one hand with the little fish still firmly attached to his thumb.

Now, people who know all about such things will tell you, "Simply relax and the fish (crab, turtle, or whatever) will then let loose." I don't doubt that wisdom in the least but have yet to find anyone who can explain how to relax with that varmint doing its best to chew your thumb off. After awhile, with Dave disturbing everyone's fishing, it didn't seem so funny, so I got a pair of pliers from the tackle box to help. We learned two things from this experience: one, two men with a pair of pliers can eventually detach an oyster fish from someone's thumb, and two, we can now recognize an oyster fish.

Deer flies are interesting little creatures, said to be capable of flying one hundred miles an hour. That speed must be a bit conservative; they would probably catch a jet if they could get inside to bite the passengers. That yellow-tinted speedster arrives, alights, and bites in a Georgia instant. You can swat, but that is usually futile; you've already been bitten. Not only speedy, he's sneaky. You may swat where he's been, and while you're swatting he has scored in a new location. The bite cannot be ignored (as with mosquitoes) since it's painful and welts will normally remain for a couple days. Accounts include near fatalities, emergency room visits, and such. Who knows? They may be true.

Some of the residents at the camp, not really having much of anything important to do and too lazy to go fishing, often gathered at one of the picnic tables in the shade of an old maple tree. To some of these characters, an invasion of deer flies was no less than a challenge. The sissies took off for screened-in areas but the stalwarts stood their ground as the air war began. Defensive weapons might include a flyswatter but normally were nothing more than a fishing cap. The deer flies always scored first and most often, but the only score kept was of deceased flies. The object was to line up eleven dead deer flies at your location on the table. With this dubious feat accomplished, you were declared an ace. Not exactly a WWI or WWII fighter plane ace but a fish camp deer fly ace nonetheless. As a general rule, these guys might have welts tomorrow but today they were feeling no pain. Yankee transplants who are always fussing about a lack of culture hereabouts might do well to investigate this sport, which is practiced nowhere else in the entire world.

Turtles come in various shapes, sizes, and colors, and it would be nice to be able to identify and describe each species. Old river rats, however, are content to know which species bite and which don't. This little bite bit concerns one alligator snapping turtle, and at the risk of rekindling old arguments, we have no alligator snapping turtles hereabouts. We do have common snapping turtles, which are distributed over a large portion of the country and may reach a weight of fifty pounds. Alligator snapping turtles are found in a smaller territory that includes northern Florida. They may exceed one hundred pounds in the wild and have been known to reach three hundred pounds in captivity.

Snapping turtles, both species, are neither pretty nor cute and, when taken from a canal or slough, do not smell like roses. One thing you must give them credit for, though, is that they are mean. And I mean *mean.* A little one just hatching, all of the size of a quarter, comes out looking for something to bite. Pick him up and he will nip the skin on your palm or fingers.

Although not recommended for everyone, a night of turtle catching can be lots of fun. Participants should try to remember that the turtles do not want to be caught and a certain amount of caution is in order. For the two involved in the following caper, the thrills of turtle catching were severely overshadowed by pain and confusion. It may well be that painkiller played a part. The problem was that the painkiller was administered preceding the pain.

Bob and his buddy Bill consistently caught huge gator turtles at one specific time during the year. Their methods were kept secret and no one was invited to join them. All we ever learned was that they fished all night and used trotlines. When they were successful, morning would find them with three or four alligator snapping turtles weighing between fifty and one hundred pounds each.

Since Bob lived on the river with his boat conveniently tied up to his dock, their turtle catching was done rather luxuriously. And although the river teemed with boaters, swimmers, and water skiers during the day, with darkness the turtle catchers had it entirely to themselves. After setting the lines and making trips to run them, they would return to Bob's house to watch TV and, of course, have a few belts of Old Stumpblower. Believe me, turtle catchers seldom had it so good.

Having already bagged two large turtles this fateful evening, Bob and Bill were running their lines again about midnight when they found they had hooked another dandy! Looked like it would go at least one hundred pounds! After considerable struggling, they managed to get the turtle into the boat. Unfortunately, Bill, perhaps a bit fatigued and possibly influenced slightly by Old Stumpblower, allowed his hand to stray a little too close. The turtle latched onto his extended index finger and neatly bit that digit off! There was momentary confusion since neither man had remotely considered such a turn of events; then Bob started the engine and headed for the house, both men doing their best to stay as far as possible from one hundred pounds of thoroughly irritated turtle. They managed to make the dock with no further damage, tied the boat up, and found a towel to wrap Bill's hand.

The dash to the emergency room provided additional thrills as Bob's car sometimes reached 100 miles per hour! To those of us who knew him well, this wasn't that amazing; Bob sometimes drove nearly that fast when he was late for work. He passed a police vehicle headed in the other direction, but this did not create any additional problems. By the time the cruiser had turned around and started pursuit, Bob and Bill had reached the hospital.

The pair received immediate attention in the emergency room. After cleaning the wound, the doctor said, "Where is the finger? We will attempt to reattach it." Bob answered in all honesty, "The last I saw of it, it was in the turtle's mouth and if you want it, you will have to go get it."

The turtle-catching episode, unfortunately, did not end at this point. As often happens with a bite from a reptile, the wound became infected and was not completely healed a year later. Bob never said what eventually happened to the turtle, but both men did give up turtle catching.

I would like to note that this incident occurred several years ago when there were no regulations protecting the alligator snapping turtle. A large, old gator turtle should never be molested. The turtles described were around long before outboard motors.

J. P.'s bite was not actually a bite; it was a sting. Of course, having been raised in Brooklyn, his outdoors education was virtually nil. He was an eager student when I tried to teach him about local wildlife and nature, though age fifty-plus is a poor time to start learning there are other creatures on earth besides humans.

J. P. had never driven a car before he escaped from Brooklyn. He somehow reached Florida, learned to drive, and became our mailman. Now, J. P. was a very pleasant fellow to talk with, and once we became acquainted he managed to take a short break and visit whenever he saw me on the porch. On one such visit, J. P. was rubbing his hand and mumbling about being bitten when he put mail in a box down the street. He hadn't really checked to see what bit him and had simply brushed the incident off. Now, however, the bite was painful and starting to swell. From what little information he could provide, it appeared that what got him was one of our plentiful little pine scorpions. I gave J. P. a fifteen-minute dissertation on what I have found in my mailbox: an entire colony of fire ants (when the area was flooded); numerous fuzzy jumping spiders; quite often a little scorpion; and once a black widow spider, which had spun its web across the opening. J. P. listened attentively, then asked, "Are they poisonous?" Sure, they're all poisonous. Most people can tolerate the bite or sting of all except the black widow with no problem. People who are highly allergic, however, must get to a doctor for a shot to counteract the effects.

The next day J. P. told me the bite had continued to swell so he had gone to the emergency room. He probably did the right thing, not knowing what reaction he might have, but this just points out one of the many disadvantages of being pen-raised on concrete.

I always try to close any session on the subject of bites by announcing, very honestly, that I am one of a very few people to have been bitten by a black bear and two jaguars.

That's a Lot of Bull

NO, THIS IS NOT OUTRIGHT CRITICISM of someone's recently told, far-fetched fish story. The title of this section is simply a first impression of a big, old Brahma. Not many of our present-day population of imported residents are intimately familiar with Brahma bulls, and that is just as well. My personal knowledge of these big fellows is also extremely limited, but that too is perfectly all right since I have no intention of keeping one as a pet, riding one to the pub, or even petting one at the zoo.

Without question, a Brahma bull looks big and is big. His rear end is about as broad as the hood on a pickup. I might add that this is the best viewpoint considering which end can do the most damage. Some have horns and others don't. It doesn't really make much difference since he's not going to honk if you are in his way. Brahma bulls certainly look lazy and they are lazy. They give the impression that they are slow, which is misleading since they are about as slow as a streak of lightning.

It may be difficult for newcomers (those who have arrived during the past thirty years) to visualize the intersection of U.S. 192 and I-95 with absolutely no buildings: no motels, no eateries, no service stations, no watering holes, no nothing. Well, that's the way it was. I-95 had been completed to U.S. 192, but there sure wasn't much traffic. Nearby were houses in West Melbourne and a large cattle pasture used by the Platt Ranch. Therein, my friends, lies the setting for some interesting memories.

I had fished till dark one night and was headed home through a neighborhood of nice houses when I suddenly found myself surrounded by a herd of cattle! Ever notice how difficult it is to see a black cow on a dark night? The huge Brahma bull, feeding on someone's lush grass, gave me only a passing glance. I eased through the cows and continued home, where I could call the police. Just because I drove thirty miles per hour didn't mean the next car wouldn't be doing sixty. No, the police were not aware of a wandering herd of cows but would check it out.

I had completely forgotten the first encounter but a couple of nights later, in the same neighborhood, there they were again. The big bull was not very sociable this time and started ambling toward the car. I was able to slip through the herd with the bull trailing behind me, then on to the house and another phone call. The police weren't the least bit surprised and knew where to find the herd. They would get right on it. I should have gone back to watch the roundup but didn't. There were plenty of cowboys living nearby, so maybe the cops just went to the nearest honky-tonk and asked for volunteers. It would have been interesting to watch.

You could sympathize with the cows. Grass in their pasture was not the best, and only a short distance away they could find lush grass, collards, radishes, carrots, tomato plants, and nice tender lettuce. It wasn't easy to build a fence that could contain a two-thousand-pound Brahma bull determined to find better eating elsewhere.

Another fishing trip, again headed home in the dark—by now, I had begun to expect seeing the herd and its leader. When I turned off 192, there he was, that big, old bull, standing with feet spread in the center of the pavement, almost as though he was waiting for me! And, let me tell you, he was mad! Driving anything less than a Sherman tank, you do not dispute the right-of-way with a Brahma bull. In a friendly mood out on the ranch, one of those suckers can do $2,000 worth of damage to your pickup just by using it for a scratching post. Maybe he recognized my car. Who knows? I put it in reverse and got out of there. Not far down 192, I noticed a police car and stopped to tell the officers the wandering herd was out again, adding, "Don't take any chances with that bull. He is irritated!"

I had only one more encounter, this one long-range, before the herd was moved to a more distant pasture. You've heard the term gun-shy? Well, I had become bull-shy. So before turning onto the herd's favorite street, I took a look. Sure enough, there were the flashing lights of two police cars.

Imagine yourself watching TV when you hear a strange noise and look outside. You see twelve cows and one enormous bull thoroughly enjoying themselves at the expense of your vegetables, flowers, grass, and shrubbery. You may chase the neighbor's cat with a broom, but if anyone tried the same method with Mr. Bull, I would liked to have watched. Of course, community attitude was much different back then, so there was no huge uproar, no lawsuits and such—only one small article in the newspaper: "Cows Invade Neighborhood Lawns." Everyone took it in stride. And there are still a few folks around who can describe the destruction of their beautiful hibiscus.

Some folks might be interested in hearing how Pepper Pete lost his little yellow airplane. It may even come as a surprise to many who knew him that Pete was once a pilot. In fact, most remember him only for his ability to grow a huge variety of hot peppers. I seem to recall Pete telling me that he flew in the Navy. Anyway, here is the little yellow airplane story.

At this particular time Pete was employed as a crop duster. Pete's airplane was one of those old Piper Cubs, which had been modified for crop dusting. The plane was yellow, a popular color for light planes, perhaps so they could more easily be located when they went down.

Pete's group had established an operating base in a pasture on the Mormon Ranch. The pasture was level, relatively free of obstructions, and quite suitable for landing small planes. The cattle didn't particularly enjoy the noise of Pete's plane and normally stayed clear of his improvised landing strip. With all necessary supplies and equipment on hand, Pete could load up, fly until his spray was exhausted, then return and repeat the process. It was a smooth and efficient operation. When he finished for the day, he tied the plane down as a precaution against our frequent little storms.

One fateful morning, as the crew approached in their pickup they could see that something did not look right. As they got closer, they could see the plane was not at all as they had left it. Friends, that plane was demolished! Torn loose from its tie downs and totally battered! Facing the plane and pawing the ground was one oversized Brahma bull!

The engine and other items were eventually salvaged from the wreckage, but the plane itself was no longer an airplane, just a pile of scrap that went to the junkyard. It was a rather costly education, to be sure, but now they knew that big Brahma bulls do not like little yellow airplanes that invade their pasture and disturb their harem.

Yankees

NOW, MOST TRANSPLANTS TO FLORIDA are fine people, and while some may adapt, blend in, and enjoy themselves a little slower than others, that's OK: they're trying. A Yankee can best be described as a person who, after being exposed to the obvious superiority of Southern living, has, unfortunately, been unable to adapt. It's a darn shame, but true Yankees appear to be miserable, always in a hurry for no apparent reason, quick to complain about anything and everything, intolerant of folks they don't know, unable to enjoy themselves, and even dissatisfied with the attraction that brought them here—the weather. Of course, everything was bigger and better in that mythical utopia the Yankee left behind, and this naturally contributes to his dissatisfaction hereabouts. Apparently the typical Yankee misses those deep snowdrifts, outrageous taxes, muggings, traffic jams, and terrific heating bills.

Yankees appear to be slow learners. This may be partially because most are along in age and we all know it is difficult to teach an old dog new tricks. Also, many Yankees feel they already possess all the knowledge they will ever need. Ignorance is excusable though sometimes embarrassing and costly.

An older gentleman Yankee, walking barefoot across his well-kept lawn, felt something prick his heel. With eyesight not the best, he thought he glimpsed a small creature disappear in the matted St. Augustine grass. Influenced by partially read newspaper articles concerning Florida's poisonous snakes, he was convinced he had been bitten by a pigmy rattler. The neighborhood was alerted, and, although no snake could be found, a volunteer offered to drive the victim to the emergency room. Examination by experienced personnel revealed only a tiny mark, no indication of a snake bite, and no symptoms. However, since the old fellow was insistent, the nurses had him take a seat in the event anything developed. Two hours later, the victim, tired of waiting but still convinced he had been bitten, decided that no venom had been injected. Back home and discussing the ordeal, the uneducated Yankee described the snake as a pigmy rattler, maybe an inch and a half long.

'Nuf said.

On the subject of driving, have a little patience. Some of these folks are like J. P., who had never driven a car until he retired at the age of fifty-five and moved to Florida. With subways and buses, J. P. had no need for a car in Brooklyn. And, if he had owned a car, parking would have cost more than his apartment.

When Yankees learn to drive, the first lesson is obviously how to use the horn. Most become experts. On the front of their Florida-registered vehicles, some like to display a car plate from that fantastic land back home. This is not compulsory although perhaps it should be. A few years back, two cars collided for no apparent reason other than that the car with the Yankee license plate had crossed the center line. Completing his accident report, the Melbourne cop was being overwhelmed by excuses from the Yankee driver when the Florida Cracker driving the other car volunteered, "It was my fault!"

Completely confused, the cop asked, "How do you figure that?"

"Well," the Cracker explained, "I saw him coming and I saw the Yankee license plate. I should have had sense enough to get out of his way!"

The subject of poorly timed traffic lights is a favorite among Yankees. Apparently, all lights are expected to turn green with the approach of important people. Maybe that old boy from New Jersey has a legitimate complaint. Lights in New Jersey are timed perfectly—a driver can go mile after mile and never have to stop. Unfortunately, we have never been able to achieve such perfection hereabouts even though local authorities hired a New Jersey traffic flow specialist some years back.

Another Yankee complaint: local seafood. This old buddy from Baltimore dearly loved crab cakes. He had ordered a crab cake at his favorite, expensive seafood restaurant and was served what he described as a crab cake unfit to eat. He voiced his dissatisfaction to the management, received an apology, and was not charged for the crab cake. The incident should have ended at this point, but, no. Whenever the subject of seafood came up at the local pub, we were to hear the same loud declaration: "Baltimore has the best seafood in the world. You can't get good seafood in this part of the country, and people around here don't even know how to make a crab cake!" Who would be the one to tell him that the owners of his seafood restaurant moved here from Baltimore and supposedly brought their crab cake expertise with them?

To his credit, this Yankee at least got out on the golf course occasionally. However, that's about as close as he would ever get to nature. Totally unfamiliar with birds, other than pigeons he had seen in parks, he asked about a large, ugly-looking bird seen on the fairways. Happy to find a Yankee with some interest in our unusual bird life, I proceeded with facts concerning the wood stork, white ibis, fish crow, and others commonly seen while golfing. I realized I was wasting my time when he pointed toward a small bird perched on a power line and asked, "What kind of bird is that?"

"That's a blackbird," I explained.

"Dammit," he said, "I didn't ask what color it was!"

Volumes could be written concerning the idiosyncrasies of Yankees, but what the heck? They complain about anything and everything and are so disagreeable you must be careful even when you're agreeing with them. Then, lo and behold, they go back home for two weeks in the summer and tell everyone about their lifestyle in Florida, where things are virtually perfect.

Wannabe Rednecks

YOU KNOW, WHEN YOU STOP TO THINK ABOUT IT, personal computers and the Internet got their start with redneck jokes. Well, I'll admit there may have been other products, but for the first year of the computer craze, all I saw were reams of redneck jokes. Computers are constantly improving, however, and redneck jokes are taking a back seat as operators move into such serious things as shopping for Limburger cheese in Paris. Admirable, but computers and stinky cheese are not the subject of this dissertation.

Rednecks are not the illiterate clods imagined in far-out redneck jokes. Those are a class of citizens with a far different definition, the use of which is now considered politically incorrect. True rednecks belong to a select group of happy-go-lucky, independent thinkers who, within reason, normally do as they please, unhindered by public opinion and unburdened by keeping up with the Joneses.

We find many bogus rednecks wearing cowboy boots and big belt buckles and driving pickup trucks. Outward appearance alone will not achieve redneckness, however! So, in the interest of helping wannabe rednecks, I offer the following observations.

You may not be a redneck if:

- You have a $20,000 fishing boat and $2,000 worth of tackle and get your fish at the market.
- You drive right past an excellent fast food joint for the privilege of standing in line for an hour at a mediocre but well-publicized restaurant.

- Your hair is so long your neck can't even get tanned.
- You work fifty weeks each year so you can have a two-week fishing vacation when the fish aren't biting.
- You've had a bad day until you manage to beat a little old lady to the last parking space in front of the drugstore.
- You can endure the customary mutilation of our national anthem before a ball game.
- You have completed sixteen years of education and don't know how to change a tire on your car.
- You don't know the words to "Dixie."
- Your pet's vet bills equal your house payments.
- You belong to a fitness club but pay someone to mow your lawn.
- You wear gold chains and other jewelry to impress everyone but impress only the criminal element.
- You smoke $4 cigars and believe Copenhagen is just a city in Denmark.
- You think Polly Esther is a fabric rather than that cute young lady you may see at the rodeo.
- You pay a miniature fortune for a TV hookup to watch one so-called boxer chew the ear of another.
- You are seen coming out of one of those $50 unisex tonsorial parlors looking like you need a haircut.
- Your idea of wildlife is to recover from one party rapidly enough to attend the next one.
- You have a billfold crammed with overworked 19% credit cards but only a total of $1.28 in cold, hard cash in your pocket.
- Your ears don't work when your mouth is flapping.
- You subscribe to the *New York Times* and don't have any mullet to wrap.
- You spend a day—most of it standing in line in the hot sun—and a bundle of money visiting one of the major local attractions, then insist you enjoyed it.
- You pay $25 for the privilege of hitting and chasing a lit-

tle white ball around a big pasture when you could have been catching fish with an investment of only $2 for bait.

- You wear shorts, shades, and white boat shoes on a cold day.
- You feel beaches shouldn't erode and floodplains shouldn't flood simply because you live there.
- You are a Florida resident who acquires a painful sunburn.
- You have an expensive, seldom-used, concrete pond in your backyard that doesn't contain one single catfish.
- You watch thoroughly rehearsed TV talk shows that insult the intelligence of most Americans.
- You feel important carrying a beeper or cell phone, useful primarily for receiving orders from your spouse.
- You brag about our beautiful beaches which, nowadays, are normally viewed through the narrow driveway between two tall condominiums.
- Your idea of roughing it is living in a large motor home with all the hookups, parked within walking distance of a restaurant, bar, theater, and massage parlor.
- You feel everything was bigger and better where you came from yet prefer not to return.
- You think you can do two things at once, like talk on the phone while driving a car.
- You pay an extra $50 to $100 for the privilege of wearing a manufacturer's logo on shoes or clothing made in a foreign country by the cheapest labor available.

Enough for now. I'm always happy to be of help. Best of luck. With perseverance, even the likes of J. P. may become successful rednecks.

Good ole J. P., a product of (and an escapee from) Brooklyn, always felt a redneck was a baseball fan who couldn't afford a good seat and consequently got his neck sunburned sitting in the cheap centerfield bleachers.

Flash

NOT TO BE CONFUSED with a late-breaking news item, this little yarn concerns a legendary fish camp dog. He was born at Lake Washington Resort and at first was accepted as just another cute puppy. His mother was a spitz and his father a bulldog, a potentially tough, mean, arrogant combination, to be sure. As fate would have it, though, and because of his choice of buddies, Flash grew up to be tough enough but definitely not mean or arrogant. He liked everyone, everyone liked him, and, quite frankly, his main concern in life was, Where is my next beer coming from? You see, Flash became a beeraholic.

When he was still quite small, Flash liked to spend his time at the bar, where he had his own private ashtray. No, he never took up smoking. The ashtray served as a bowl where his buddies would share their beer. Perhaps smarter than his benefactors, Flash knew his limits even as a puppy. Many early mornings he might be seen, staggering a bit as he made his way out the door and across the driveway searching for a shady spot to sleep it off.

Flash grew rapidly and obviously felt he was one of the boys. When invited, he would hop up onto a bar stool, sit there like any other paying customer, and wait to have his ashtray filled. Weighing maybe sixty pounds, his agility was amazing. Lord knows what strangers thought when treated to such a performance.

Flash didn't spend all his time in the bar and might sometimes be seen wandering the area doing doggie things. Whenever I mowed or cleaned up the wildlife park, I could expect him to show up. At first, I was foolish enough to think he came to see me. Not so. That rascal was only interested in my open can of beer sitting on the picnic table. One time, I was working alone when here came Flash, wagging his stubby tail as best he could and downright happy to see me. All this attention was unusual—I wasn't one of his favorite people because I never gave him any beer. I continued to work and Flash soon disappeared into the underbrush. Sometime later, being a firm believer in an occasional beer break, I sat down at the picnic table and reached for my open can. Whoops! The can was overturned and there was no puddle of beer. Not giving it much thought, I assumed the can had been nearly empty and a wind gust had blown it over. I took a couple of sips from a fresh beer and went back to work. Thirty minutes later as an unpaid laborer with no boss—it was time for another break. Surprise, surprise! That fresh can of beer was also overturned with no indication of a spill. I hadn't seen the unusually friendly Flash for a while. Not willing to risk my third and last can of beer, I left it unopened on the table while I pretended to work. A short time later, as if on cue, Flash emerged from the brush and quietly hopped up onto the table. Caught in the act, Flash appeared to be embarrassed as he looked first at me, then longingly at the beer before hopping down to amble off toward the bar.

It was well worth the price of a couple beers to learn how that cunning canine operated. His modus operandi would certainly remain secret with me. Many were the times I watched people at the horseshoe pits get blamed for spilling a beer while Flash innocently sat by, licking his chops and planning his next move.

While it might appear that Flash really didn't amount to much, such was not the case. In spite of being a beer guzzler, he did everything expected of him. He was the best snake-catching dog I have ever seen in action. Believe me, he lived up to his name. He moved like a flash!

Flash wasn't fully grown when he had his first moccasin encounter. He won, of course, but became so sick from the snake's bites it looked like he might become a loser. Fortunately, the only lasting effect was an intense hatred for all snakes, developed while he lay around all day with his jaw swollen to twice its normal size.

After that, Flash's snake fights became frequent. He hunted them and seemed to specialize in cottonmouths. I never knew him to get by without being bitten, but as time went by he developed an immunity and the effects became less severe. He loved to go airboating, and, if the boat pulled up onto dry land, Flash was off hunting before the boat fully stopped. Fellow riders need not watch for snakes; Flash had swept the area.

Now, if you want to liven up a dull gathering of regular fish camp patrons, just introduce a snake to the scene. There were six people, totally inactive and maybe half asleep, when someone spotted a snake slithering alongside the bait tank. I had been through similar exhibitions before and knew the proper way to react: just pick the most distant barstool, get your feet up out of the way, and hope for the best. The five others grabbed anything handy—a mop, a broom, and three pool cues—and started flailing away. Chances of being bitten by the snake were almost nil, but the likelihood of being bashed by a pool cue was very nearly certain.

Turmoil deluxe: everyone dashing about, swinging away, shouting instructions, a little profanity, and an occasional, "Ouch." It went on for maybe ten minutes while I sipped my beer and ducked an occasional wild swing. Then Jack Jr. became a little sensible. He held the door open and shouted, "Flash! Snake!"

The speed of that dog never ceased to amaze me. Although he was half hung-over and had been sleeping in the shade when he got the call, he was inside in about four bounds, crunching the snake in his bulldog jaws. Oh, yes, it was a cottonmouth, and, as usual, Flash was bitten. All in a day's work for Flash. When convinced the snake was thoroughly deceased, he carried it outside, dropped it, and resumed his nap.

Flash and Lenny became friends because Flash, of course,

liked everyone and perhaps saw Lenny as a potential beer-buying buddy. Anyway, Flash's efforts left a lasting impression—and maybe a few scratches—on Lenny.

This fine summer day, Lenny, his wife, and her little dog, Bandit, went out for a ride and decided to visit Lake Washington Resort. Lenny was parking his pickup when Flash wandered onto the scene, obviously determined to act as a one-dog reception committee. That rascal, standing flat-footed, jumped through the open passenger side window without touching the truck!

Now, Flash was no puny little critter. He was sixty pounds of well-muscled bulldog, and, as you might imagine, the cab of Lenny's pickup suddenly became more than a little crowded. Lenny's wife and Bandit were willing to give up their seats. (There is some question as to whether Bandit or Lenny's wife was first to find the door handle. No matter—both hit the ground on a dead run.) Lenny himself would have liked to bail out had not Flash come to rest firmly wedged between Lenny and the steering wheel. Always extremely friendly, Flash showed he could also be affectionate as he thoroughly licked Lenny's face.

Lenny felt diplomacy was the best approach to the situation. He would just turn the cab over to Flash if he could edge his way out the door. It worked and there sat Flash in complete control. I want to remind you: Flash's expressions were almost human. Looking a bit dejected and certainly unhappy that these folks didn't want to associate with him, Flash hopped out of the truck and ambled off toward the bar, where he knew he had friends.

Flash's demise came suddenly and unexpectedly. Early one morning, as Sharon was going to work, he dashed in front of her car. The accident proved to be fatal. There was no logical explanation for Flash's carelessness, though we might assume he had seen a snake in the headlights. It was a day of mourning as the fish camp had lost perhaps its most interesting family member. Without ceremony, Chuck and Hippie Steve buried Flash on the mound behind Jack's house. He would be sorely missed by all who knew him.

Others might not agree, but I believe Flash gained a bit of notoriety some ten years later while the old fish camp property was being developed into a county park. During excavation, a backhoe operator partially exposed what appeared to be a skull and some ribs. Never examined closely enough for definite identification, the remains, accepted as an ancient Indian burial, were simply covered up. In approximately the same location and depth as Flash's grave, the remains, I am convinced, were those of our beer-drinking, snake-catching favorite dog.

Airboating is Fun!

MISCHIEVOUS AIRBOATERS might at times create minor disturbances. They might even do something not totally in compliance with our many laws and ordinances. Most of us view these transgressions in the same manner as a politician pilfering public funds: if they get away with it, it must be OK.

Bob and some of his buddies had made a night of airboating. About 1:00 A.M. they called it quits, loaded their boats, and headed for town. An all-night restaurant looked mighty inviting to the crew since they'd had nothing to eat all night. So Bob whipped in and parked his rig out of everyone's way.

After everyone had finished eating around 2:00 A.M., the night's activities would normally have concluded, except a group of bikers roared up to the restaurant. Everyone knows motorcycles don't have to be loud and noisy, but then what's the use of owning a big, old, classy hog if you can't attract attention? Anyway, Bob, having been a biker himself, casually nodded, then couldn't resist the temptation. "If you think those bikes are noisy, you ain't heard nothin' yet."

Well, one thing led to another, and the visiting bikers, being totally unfamiliar with airboats, became curious. Nothing for Bob to do but demonstrate that, as noise-makers, motorcycles are minor league! The bikers' education could have ended at this point and we would have no story. However, Bob, with such an appreciative audience, offered one of them a ride. The absence of water was somewhat of a handicap, of course, but there *was* that dirt alley alongside the restaurant.

The bikers may have had misgivings, but not Bob. He knew his boat would perform just as well at 2:00 A.M. in a quiet residential neighborhood as it would out on the river. With only two onboard, the boat fairly flew to the end of the alley and back. The entire biker group was downright impressed, and now more wanted a ride. With two, three, four, or more riders, the trip was a blast (in more ways than one). Eventually, though, with twelve bikers hanging on to any handhold they could find, the overloaded boat refused to budge. OK, it was time to quit anyway. Bob loaded the boat and bid all his new-found biker friends goodnight as he headed home. What stories those bikers would have to tell when they returned to Paducah.

No harm, no foul. Right? Well, let's see.

Some of the boys, speculating on what may have happened had a city policeman chanced upon the scene of this activity, drew up a list of potential charges:

1. Operating unlicensed vehicle on a public thoroughfare
2. No headlights
3. No taillights
4. No brake lights
5. No turn signals
6. Operating overloaded watercraft
7. Insufficient personal flotation devices
8. Open containers (empty beer cans)

It was a very impressive list so they took it a step further and created a fake arrest report as it would have appeared in the newspaper with the culprit's name intentionally blacked out. They went to a lot of trouble, but in the end their report was very authentic looking.

At the next unofficial meeting of the has-been river rats, Bob was presented with the fake arrest report and everyone had a good laugh. Bob put the clipping in his pocket, intending to show his wife. Since she worked at the hospital until 2:00 A.M., he just left it on the countertop in the kitchen when he went to bed.

Well, shortly after 2:00 A.M. Bob was rudely awakened by a seriously irritated Mrs. Bob, waving what appeared to be an authentic newspaper Crime Line report. Of course, Bob's explanation wasn't very convincing since he was half asleep. But Mrs. Bob persisted until Bob, now fully awake, told Mrs. Bob to call his rabble-rousing buddies who had caused this calamity, then retired to the living room to sleep on the couch.

The Last Resort

OLD TIMEY FISH CAMPS, AS WE KNEW AND LIKED THEM, were destined for extinction, like two-for-a-nickel cigars, ten-cent draft beer, and gasoline at twenty-five cents per gallon. When it got to the point where a fish camp operator could make more money driving a truck for the county than he made working twelve hours a day trying to maintain an enjoyable old fish camp, it was time to quit. Some camps simply disappeared while others survived by converting to tourist attractions with airboat rides, restaurants, and such. These survivors may still bear the title "fish camp," but little else remains. Find me one where you can loaf around for an afternoon, visit with old buddies, retell fish stories, drink a couple of beers, play a couple of games of pool, then get your boat out of its stall for some relaxed fishing, all without a loud jukebox blaring and the beer maid urging you to drink up. If there is such a place, it must be a private club with membership dues higher than my exorbitant property taxes.

For several years, the renters at Lake Washington Resort had been hand-picked—retirees and others who kept a low profile and made little disturbance. Closing time for the camp, normally 9:00 or 10:00 in the evening, depended upon how many were present. Most everyone knew everyone else, and the few strangers who made an appearance did not normally remain strangers for long.

There were occasional free feeds, normally on weekends. These might feature turtle, fish, venison, and sometimes swamp cabbage. Everyone was welcome at these events, which permitted our amateur cooks an opportunity to show off their outstanding skills. You could count on an abundance of food, the likes of which could not be duplicated in any restaurant.

Benefits sponsored by the Lake Washington Conservation Association always produced excellent results, thanks to an abundance of hard-working volunteers. An indication of the popularity of these events is that it was sometimes necessary to run a shuttle service nearly to I-95.

The fish camp crowd was a group of generous, friendly folks, almost like one big happy family. While the patrons were quite content, however, Lake Washington Resort itself was not overly prosperous. Over a period of time, necessary maintenance was neglected. Then Jane, attempting to manage the resort on her own, became hospitalized and passed away. With permanent closure of the camp looming, the property was purchased by Jack Harnish.

Things would never be the same around the old fish camp. Needed repairs were started immediately and a new, larger bar built. Those old leaky roofs were repaired and fresh paint applied. The population of the camp increased considerably, as did the beer consumption. Some of these newcomers worked, some worked part-time, and some didn't seem concerned about working. The only remaining long-time residents, Ernie and Harold, often had their sleep interrupted while the other rental cabins appeared to have a constant turnover of occupants. We old-timers soon learned that our loafing time around the camp was restricted to mornings and early afternoons. The newcomers, basically likable people, apparently felt every evening was party time. For many obvious reasons, we few remaining long-time river rats felt justified in sometimes calling Lake Washington Resort the "last resort."

Dickie, arriving from somewhere, became a prominent resident of the resort. Dickie drove a Buick that at one time had been a nice-looking car. Easily recognized, the Buick looked as though it had been through one or more demolition derbies. It had an unbelievable collection of dents and scratches with more added daily. It even had dents in the roof, which only Dickie could explain. Not particularly a hazard on the highway, Dickie specialized in innocent, inanimate, stationary objects. You know, things like telephone poles, sign posts, the sides of buildings, and objects of that nature. Dickie's cabin was only about three hundred feet from the entrance to the fish camp. One memorable day, before finally getting parked in his normal space and shutting off the engine, he had managed to hit six separate inanimate and inoffensive objects. Dickie's name is in the record book—not for the largest fish, the biggest buck, or the best in horseshoe-throwing, but for this one-of-a-kind feat.

Good old Bob, nowadays reformed and well-behaved, earned a dubious reputation for turning off the electricity. If the lights went out, the TV set went off, the noisy jukebox quieted, and the cash register quit working, someone would invariably comment, "Looks like Bob is on his way home." Truthfully, it is not especially unusual for someone to knock down a power pole, is it? Well, how about the same pole on two separate occasions? Friends, that is a distinctive accomplishment.

Then there was the magnetic oak tree. About a quarter mile down the road, on a slight bend and off to the right, was a medium-size oak. Harmless-looking and well off the roadway, you would never expect it to attract so many vehicles. There are about a dozen in my memory. The tree never suffered anything more than some scarred bark, but the vehicles normally required a tow. Wish I could have been there when the county removed the tree; it surely contained a huge magnet. They should have replaced that oak with a rubber tree.

One of the women at the camp, staying in the cabin nearest the road, had the advantage of a private parking space between the house and canal. There was plenty of space for most drivers to park there, but one day she made a slight miscalculation, turned off the road too soon, and drove directly into the canal. It must have been a rude awakening to find herself abruptly surrounded by water. No permanent damage, however, since the canal was only about two feet deep at the time.

You'd have to admit, C. C. was an unusual old boy. Barefoot and wearing bib overalls, he may have looked the part but he wasn't a Florida Cracker by any stretch of the imagination,. C. C. was normally pretty well-behaved, but around 2:00 one morning he broke one of the camp's few rules: No shooting in the compound. Now, 2:00 A.M. is not usually a good time to discuss rules and regulations with anyone who seems to have plenty of ammunition and no particular target. The next day, however, when C. C. wandered into the bar, Jack Jr. took the time to explain this simple policy designed to preserve life and limb.

"By the way, what in the world were you shooting at?" Jack asked.

"I was shootin' coconuts out of the palm trees," C. C. replied.

"There aren't any coconuts in those cabbage trees."

"Wow, I must have got 'em all!"

So this was the final chapter in the history of Lake Washington Resort, which ended abruptly with the purchase of the property for a county park. Boat stalls were rapidly vacated, and the many tenants scrambled to find new living quarters. A few of us old-timers and some former residents moved our inactivity (loafing) to the pub, which we tried to rename Lake Washington Resort East. It wasn't the same, of course, but we had a fresh group of listeners when we got carried away telling of our many exploits on the river.

The Upper St. Johns River

IN WRITING ABOUT THE UPPER ST. JOHNS RIVER, it is impossible to avoid comparing present-day conditions to those of the past. The following, therefore, may sound like a series of complaints, and perhaps that is exactly what it is.

Understandably, a newcomer treated to an extensive airboat ride on any part of the Upper St. Johns River would enthusiastically declare the area to be naturally wild, beautiful, and virtually unspoiled. Those of us who have been here for awhile would agree that it is still beautiful, but certainly not natural or unspoiled.

A serious fisherman, viewing the river for the first time, would see an endless expanse of potentially perfect fishing territory. Most of us old-timers, who for years enjoyed superb fishing, no longer even participate in the sport.

This young, interesting, intelligent couple, freshly arrived from somewhere up north, heaped compliment after compliment on the appearance of Lake Washington, saying it was the most beautiful wild, natural lake they had ever see. After some several minutes of this admiration, the young lady innocently asked, "But, where are all the houses?" Obviously, where they were from, it was expected that the beautiful, wild, natural aspects of any lake would be destroyed by surrounding it with houses.

There are numerous local bass tournaments with sometimes as many as 150 to 200 participants. They catch a few small fish and may, on rare occasions, catch one of decent size. Now here are 150 to 200 fishermen evidently quite content to catch small bass in waters that, for many years, were notorious for bass of ten pounds or more.

Conditions on the river were not always perfect even in the old days. There were floods, droughts, hyacinths, and, very rarely, a fish kill. So what is the difference nowadays? Well as simple as it can be explained—conditions on the river were not always perfect then, but conditions on the river are never perfect today. There is a difference.

Lake Hellen Blazes has had a glorious past, with an emphasis on past. For many years Lake Hellen enjoyed the reputation of being among the finest bass fishing lakes in the entire country. At times, it was indeed the very best.

As recent as 1966-1967 the lake contained a large population of bass, many of which were trophy size. Water depth exceeded six feet in places and hyacinths were the only troublesome vegetation. When weather conditions were reasonable, Lake Hellen would produce a bass of eight or more pounds each fishing trip.

Hyacinths, considered a nuisance, actually added intrigue. They normally covered one fourth of the lake surface and drifted where the wind dictated. With a strong wind from the south, there was no possibility of fishing the lake—the entrance would be totally blocked. At other times, with light winds, the hyacinth were not densely packed, and with patience a boat could be worked through them. Under these conditions a constant watch for wind change was maintained, and if the wind freshened, a dash for the opening was necessary. Trapped behind a sheet of packed-in hyacinths, with the small opening solidly plugged, you would be in serious trouble.

In more recent years there have been periods when Lake

Hellen Blazes produced fish, not of the size or amount as before, but enough to indicate the lake was trying to come back. Low water, fish kills, and other hazards halted each of these efforts.

A visit to Hellen Blazes now leaves a person extremely discouraged. What is normally seen is a shallow, muck-filled, hydrilla-choked mud hole with virtually no fish and no semblance of its former glory. How about that? The lake went from having the best bass fishing in the country to having zero bass fishing in such a short period of time!

Golfers and golf courses seem to get a great deal of attention nowadays, so perhaps a comparison is in order. To a golfer, this situation would equate to converting his favorite golf course to a garbage dump. He might play around the discarded refrigerators and trash for awhile, but eventually would be unable to find the greens.

Lake Sawgrass, like Hellen Blazes, was a beautiful lake that also provided years and years of outstanding fishing. Just a short run from the fish camp, it was an ideal place to fish when you didn't have much time or the weather was iffy. A thousand true fishing tales could be told of Lake Sawgrass—ten-pound bass, stringers of speckled perch, large shellcrackers, turtles, catfish—but they all add up to a comparison of what was to what is. Making such comparisons, one can only become irritated and completely underwhelmed by the feeble efforts and excuses offered for the condition of the St. Johns River!

Enough of that—let me tell of two interesting Lake Sawgrass events.

The first, back about 1966, somehow went unnoticed. And, as we shall see, this was perfectly all right with those principally involved since they, obviously, weren't seeking publicity.

At the time, except for a small area on the north end, Sawgrass was completely choked with vegetation. Not simply floating hyacinths and such, there was an accumulation of everything that might wash down the river. All this was packed in so tightly that it actually acted as a dam, allowing the river current only to seep through. The lake had been in this condition for some time and the situation worsened as more material continued to pack in with that already there. There was no telling how long it'd been since a kicker boat was able to travel south.

I was fishing Lake Washington when there was a tremendous explosion somewhere down south. Now, with an explosion of that magnitude, I was almost certain a disaster had occurred somewhere. No smoke was visible to pinpoint the location, but I expected sirens and possibly planes overhead at any time. Listening intently, thirty minutes passed and nothing of that sort happened. The only noticeable change was in the fish. Bass that had been hitting reasonably well suddenly stopped. Evidently the concussion had sent them all into hiding.

As the day wore on, I worked my way south and eventually to Sawgrass, the explosion all but forgotten. To my complete surprise, out there in the middle of the lake was a large boat with a seventy-five-horse-power motor, tearing back and forth, trying to maintain an open trail through that mass of vegetation! All this activity was a mystery, but after awhile the others noticed my boat and came alongside to ask if I would run through that mess to keep it open while they went to get more boats. They explained that they had set off half a case of dynamite to clear the trail, and if I could keep it open, they would soon be back with several boats to get all that vegetation moving out.

As we always remarked in those days, we would send it all to Jacksonville. It is doubtful that any of the mess ever made it that far, but those were our intentions nonetheless. It was a pretty difficult-looking job for my small ten-horse motor, but what the heck. The trick was to keep that stuff moving without becoming trapped. At the middle I'd be two or three hundred yards from open water. Fortunately, everything went well, though my unknown friends and their flotilla of boats never did return. No telling what type of disaster those fellows ran into, maybe a pool game or something equally important, but quite alone with darkness coming on, I quit.

The lake-clearing operation was successful beyond all expectations. Two days later, Lake Sawgrass was, once again, a wide-open body of water with only scattered patches of water lilies. All this accomplished by four men with two boats and a borrowed half case of dynamite—no local, state, or federal aid involved. Not a single dead fish was sighted and the blast provided benefits for years to come.

It is doubtful that anyone else noticed the additional benefits of the dynamite blast. There was now a deep hole in the center of the lake, which because of its depth and clear sand bottom, became home territory for all the large bass. They spawned on that clean bottom and retreated to the deep hole when water temperatures were down. I suppose all good things must come to an end, so over the years the hole filled with muck and became no more attractive than the rest of the lake bottom.

The second unusual Sawgrass incident occurred at the site of the dynamite blast. My fishing lure had become hung on an object where there should have been no obstructions. Curious, I moved the boat closer to discover a string of fish traps.

Through the clear water, I could see the traps had been abandoned for a long time, since under the traps were the bones of many fish and turtles that had starved or drowned, then rotted away and fell through the wire mesh. Nearly all of the traps still contained live fish, all of which were in poor condition.

If nothing else, this was a learning experience. The traps that held catfish contained nothing else. The traps that held bass contained numerous small bream. Apparently bass would not feed while confined in the traps but catfish would continue to feed as long as anything was available.

This string of traps, abandoned for two months, had for some reason continued to catch fish and there is no way of knowing how many fish they killed. Perhaps all the fish that were released survived, but again who knows? One very large catfish, nothing but skin and bones, was still quite active. A large bass that should have weighed nine pounds was in the same condition and I doubted it would survive. It may be noted that, having been cut into very small pieces, the traps presented no further hazard to the fish population.

Long before the invasion of hydrilla, hyacinths were considered an immense, uncontrollable problem. This they were, but today's hydrilla problems tend to make everyone forget the things we complained so bitterly about years ago.

Hyacinths floated and were moved about by wind and the river current. They would sometimes pack so densely that a lightweight person could walk on them. They could effectively plug boat ramps, boat stalls, narrow openings and passageways, at times preventing kicker boat traffic completely. When they were at their worse, little could be done. Spraying would kill them, but the hyacinths were still there until they rotted or were moved out by current or the wind. With conditions perfect you could sometimes clear an area by pushing them with a boat. What you got rid of became someone else's problem further north.

A few scattered hyacinths were beneficial, their roots dangling two feet below the water surface provided a hiding place for minnows, freshwater shrimp, eels, and such. A trick few fishermen ever learned was to run their boat into the downwind side of packed hyacinths and disturb small clumps, which would then drift away. This stirred up the hidden baitfish and usually created a brief feeding frenzy. A small lure fished properly could pick up a couple of bass before the activity slowed. Then you simply repeated the process of disturbing the hyacinths and added a few more bass to your catch. These were not large-sized bass, the big ones being loners, but it was a surefire method of catching a mess of eating-sized fish in a short period of time.

The hyacinth problem now seems to have been whipped by an imported insect. There are still a few around, but no one should fuss about a few hyacinths.

Extensive periods of consistently high water don't happen often and even brief periods are genuinely appreciated. When the marshes flood, all wildlife flourishes. The fish, fanning out over new territory, find an abundance of food, reproduction increases, and the tiny fry grow rapidly. Under ideal conditions hereabouts, bass will grow to ten or twelve inches during their first year. Birds return and they too have plenty of food. Gators can roam to their hearts content, and no doubt even the snakes prosper.

There is also the occasional flood. Generally speaking, flooding on the river is beneficial. This of course is not a viewpoint shared by some of the dry-land wildlife and folks foolish enough to live in or on the edge of the floodplain.

Beaches have always eroded and floodplains have always flooded, so little sympathy is wasted on those who choose to live in such locations.

One year a flood managed to cover the entire area, with the help of a hurricane. Airboats could travel virtually anywhere while kicker boats could run the marshes and reach many of the normally inaccessible sites. The water had inched up on what was normally the riverbank, then into the parking area, and eventually, up to the porch steps. The camp was built on pilings, but even then the water came within inches of the floor and the parking area was under two feet of water.

There was little reason to fish since the fish were now scattered over many thousands of acres. Boat rides produced some unusual sights however. Snakes that had been flooded out were searching for high ground or anything they could crawl on to get out of the water—they would crawl in your boat if given a chance. I stopped at a tiny island to count the marooned rabbits and found more than a hundred in an area half the size of a tennis court. The elevated roadbed of Route 192 became a temporary refuge for thousands of rabbits and other wildlife. As might be expected, several folks came out from town to hunt rabbits, although "hunt" is probably not the correct term since they carried only a broomstick and a croaker sack. The hunters, to be sure, were watchful for snakes, which were nearly as numerous as the rabbits.

It did seem rather strange to come in from a boat ride and tie up to the porch steps where you could unload without getting your feet wet.

There was little activity on the river other than airboaters, who had a ball going anyplace that wasn't fenced, and even some fenced areas where the fence was underwater.

Floating islands of all shapes and sizes crammed the river run. It was interesting to watch them float by, pushed along by the strong current of the flooded river, some carrying a variety of wildlife and the larger ones covered with bushes and trees. One lone squirrel came ashore at the camp, where it surely must have felt isolated. Other than the few trees at the camp, there were none within a mile. The islands were basically large clumps of peat that had been above water long enough to dry out and produce trees or other vegetation. They were buoyant and simply floated when the water level became high enough to break them loose. We at the camp recognized some of these islands. You knew where they came from by the vegetation they carried and it made a lasting impression when an island next to which you had caught a nine-pound bass two weeks earlier floated past.

All this didn't seem amazing to us locals, but it would have been interesting to get the impression of a stranger, watching an island with rabbits, snakes, and a ten-foot tree float by.

Riding the river current some fifteen miles or so, most of the islands found their way no farther than Lake Washington, where they blew around for awhile and eventually eroded away to become muck on the lake bottom.

There will be more floods, as there always have been. And while the negative aspects will again get all of the attention, the many benefits will go unnoticed.

Even brief dry spells play havoc with the river and marshes, but sure enough, a drought causes damage that takes years to recover.

Just a thought—there seem to have been extended periods of low water during the time of the ancient Indians, since concentrations of artifacts are sometimes found at locations that would normally be underwater.

Few people who now regularly use Lake Washington for recreation realize that not a great many years back the water was so low a person could walk across the lake. No one did, but there were volunteers with the provision that the event be recorded on film. Boaters who sometimes find fault with the county launching ramp should have seen it then. It was nearly a hundred yards from the ramp to the water. The few who launched backed their trailers out on the sandy lake bottom and hoped they wouldn't get stuck. Most did, however.

Someone should have gotten a photograph of Lefty mowing the lake bottom. His was the only house on Lake Washington, so as the water receded and weeds sprung up, he simply mowed the area from his bulkhead to the water. Another unusual picture would have been the big old water gauge, its pilings anchored there in the dry sand, with no water near it.

The drought did not occur overnight of course. With a slight drop in water level each day there was little cause for alarm, but when this continued day after day for weeks, then months, the impending disaster was obvious. Before the drought, there had been several years of reasonably high water, making natural conditions near perfect. Fish and wildlife had prospered unbelievably, then day by day conditions deteriorated.

As the water level continued to fall, the fish moved from south to north, seeking enough water for survival. First they vacated Hellen Blazes, all those big bass moving through the river run to Little Sawgrass, which had a bit more depth though not much.

For a period of time, one small patch of lilies in Little Sawgrass contained virtually every large bass that had migrated from further south. Perhaps seventy-five feet in diameter, lilies within the patch moved constantly from bass brushing against them.

A cast into any part of the lily patch produced an immediate strike by a bass seven pounds or larger. Those fish were packed in so tightly, with little natural food remaining, they would hit any sort of lure. Each time out I stopped by to catch one big bass for display and release at the camp. Other than that, the spot was kept secret for fear of someone wiping out that concentration of huge bass. This, you might say, was wishful thinking. With no attention whatsoever from fishermen, very, very few of those large bass were to survive.

As the water receded further, those same fish had to move on to Lake Sawgrass, then the deep hole at Route 192, and survivors eventually on to Lake Washington.

During this time the hot stagnant water was taking its toll. Forage food had been exhausted. What should have been nine- or ten-pound bass were reduced to skeletons of seven pounds or less and all remaining fish were covered with serious fungus infections.

This, the worst of all fish kills, went practically unnoticed since it was not one massive occurrence. Fish died daily from infections and such, and as they sank or floated, their remains were immediately cleaned up by the many scavengers. There was hardly any reason to fish. Fish that were caught put up no fight and were in such poor condition they were not worth cleaning. All wildlife suffered, not only the fish. Gators? Of course the big ones survived, but perhaps at the expense of smaller ones. Wading birds? Wading birds require marshes and there were no marshes, only dried out peat bogs. Wading birds have never regained the number that once existed. No longer do you see a flight of white ibis temporarily obscure the sun like a cloud.

There are aftershocks of that recent drought. Would you believe there are enough concrete blocks on the bottom of Lake Washington to build a two-story house or small condo? Lost boat anchors were abundant. One thing some of us will regret—we did not think to search that clean sand bottom for Indian artifacts. They may just have been abundant too.

The Upper St. Johns River is indeed tough. It will rebound from all adversity. Take away the problems and it will immediately revert to producing fish and returning to being a one-of-a-kind natural wonder of Florida.

It took time of course, but once again there were ten-pound bass and a determined effort by the other wildlife. All this in preparation for the next catastrophe.

A relatively new, but serious, problem is hydrilla. Some of the old-timers may recall with amusement two patches of eel grass. Both of these patches were small, one located between Lake Washington and Lake Winder, and the other south of Little Sawgrass. Outboard props often became entangled in the grass and the operator would have to stop and clear the prop. You might, in fact, have to clean your prop twice before getting through a patch. Believe me, there was some cussin' and fussin' over those two small patches. Well, it is doubtful if either patch now exists, probably choked out by hydrilla. But that's not the worst of it. Nowadays no one cusses the eel grass since, with thousands of acres of matted hydrilla, you can seldom reach either of the locations by kicker boat.

A great deal of money is being spent in an attempt to discover a means of controlling this exotic weed, thus far without much success—chemicals, weed-eating fish, and now, an insect. Neighbors with small private ponds first used chemicals and, if administered properly, this temporarily controlled the hydrilla. The weed soon recovered however, requiring continued applications. Next it was weed-eating fish. These fish are great—they will eat the hydrilla and grow and grow. They will also eat lilies and any other vegetation in your pond. One neighbor, when there was nothing left for the fish to eat, fed his grass clippings.

Feeling that a little hydrilla may benefit the fish, I clean my pond with a garden rake. If an area is cleared down to the clean sand, it takes the hydrilla quite some time to become reestablished. Seems the plants needs a little sediment to get started again.

Could this principle be applied to a body of water where chemicals should not be used? Lake Washington for example. A small, comparatively inexpensive suction dredge could clear, at least on the perimeter of the lake, and deposit the hydrilla and sediment some distance from the shoreline. The fish would certainly appreciate some clean sand bottom and it might benefit the city water plant. It is probably impossible—too costly, permits could not be obtained, the water plant might be affected. Yet it is interesting to make a comparison—we have the expertise to maintain huge harbors, ports, and inland waterways, but are completely baffled when it comes to cleaning weeds and muck from the bottom of tiny Lake Washington.

Shucks, I don't know. I can't even spell enjunear.

Saltwater, like various chemicals, will kill hydrilla. And apparently a low content of salt will do the job. Those tributaries of the river with sufficient salt content contain no hydrilla. Hydrilla in ponds fed by flowing wells will disappear when the salt content of the well water reaches a certain point. No noticeable effect on the fish, but the weed is gone.

Saltwater is free and plentiful. Transportation would involve some costs, but if we can pump drinking water to the beaches, we could certainly pump ocean water to the river.

Oh well, just another thought, for whatever it is worth.

Of all the problems facing the river, fish kills are the least acceptable. The current trend is to label fish kills as natural and unavoidable. Well, many of us who have spent a great deal of time on the river find them unacceptable, unnatural, and avoidable.

Few people bother to investigate fish kills and there is very little impact from reading newspaper accounts. Even pictures do not tell the story. As a result, some few days after the odor of decaying fish subsides, you will once again see people fishing and actually expecting to catch fish. Six months later you may talk to experienced fishermen who tried every trick, but still could not catch fish they were certain were there. Most refuse to believe that the fish they are after were consumed by buzzards, gators, and coons, or simply rotted away six months earlier. Unfortunately, where there may have been a thousand fish, there may now be only five.

Everyone with any interest in the river should make an effort to see the results of a fish kill. First you will see the buzzards, and normally they won't be feeding. Carrion is so plentiful the birds are stuffed within minutes and spend most of their time perched on fence posts or other handy objects. Next will be the windrows of dead and bloated fish—large, small, and every size between, the fish kills plays no favorites. Some fish kills last a long time—a recent one lasting for more than a week. When this happens, you will see fish in the process of dying on the borderline of the killer water. Fish will go up canals and ditches in an attempt to find water they can survive in. That time there was such an influx of killer water it simply followed them up their retreats.

A fish kill is not a pretty sight and it just might make you mad. Most folks will feel more concern over a bloated eight-pound bass than a four-inch brim, but one thing is for certain, neither of them will contribute to repopulating the river. Some few may escape while others will migrate into the affected area, and so starts another, quite likely futile effort to return to normal. During this process one thing is vividly clear—there are few big fish. If a fish kill claims all the eight- to ten-pound bass, those fish were probably seven or eight years old. So when this happens, you can only hope that there are no more fish kills, and then with eight years of patience, there may once again be some large bass.

Viewing a fish kill, you might ask, "Why bag and size limits?" One single fish kill will often destroy more fish than have been harvested by fishermen over the previous ten years. There are many local bass tournaments and from newspaper reports, few fish are caught. This does not reflect on the contestants—there are few fish. With a fish kill, the windblown, bloated fish tend to gather in various locations—enough dead bass in an area ten feet by ten feet to have won most any local tournament plus big bass honors. Those fish will not be available for the next tournament!

A year or so after a major fish kill you may read of a minor fish kill. What could it be other than minor? There were few fish left to die!

In my opinion, not much can be done about floods, but fish kills can be stopped. And so it is that many of us old codgers, feeling conditions on the river could, and should, be improved, find ourselves hopelessly outnumbered by the uninterested, the uninformed, and those quite content with things as they are.

Concluding Remarks

TIME FLIES WHEN YOU'RE HAVING FUN. The St. Johns River, lakes, fish camps, and people provided an abundance of this necessary ingredient.

Our old buddy Duke, a true gentleman blessed with better-than-average common sense, has not been with us for a few years. However, Duke left behind one logical bit of advice he believed in and lived by: "Sure, things have changed and we don't like it! Quit complaining and enjoy what's left!"

So fishing is not what it once was. To a good fisherman, this should present only a challenge. All the thoroughly desirable features are still there: the river, lakes, marshes, and wildlife. Boat traffic may be a bit trying on weekends, but then weekday mornings were always the best choice. What can be more enjoyable than an airboat ride with buddies across the lake, over the dam, and through the river run to the Oak Head? We enjoyed a couple of hours of relaxed conversation, and perhaps someone thoughtfully brought snacks. No matter that fishing and hunting tales may have become slightly exaggerated over the years. World problems? An assemblage of old river rats in the delightful atmosphere of the Oak Head can solve them all.

Wildlife sightings, of course, are dependent upon the season, the weather, and other factors. Except during the coldest weather, gators will be seen. We don't recognize many individually, but when a twelve-footer slides off the bank, we might remember that we've been observing that now-boss gator since he was a little fellow only a foot long.

Deer and turkeys are still with us in spite of hunting pressure. Approaching such places as the Oak Head, you may see both or at least find their tracks in sandy spots not covered with vegetation. Marsh and wading birds, perhaps not as abundant as we would like, are always present. The common gallinule, that bird that frequents all airboat trails, dodging out of the way at the last second, sometimes appears to be having a population explosion.

There you have it. Things could be better and they could be worse. Perhaps everything we old river rats enjoyed is still available in smaller portions.

Lake Washington County Park, constructed at the site of the former Lake Washington Resort.